Miles Gibson was born in the New Forest in 1947. He was educated at Sandhills Primary School (where he learned to cut things out with plastic scissors) and Somerford Secondary School (where he lost a curious number of plimsolls.). Two collections of his poetry have been published and he writes, sometimes, for the *Telegraph* Sunday Magazine. He lives alone in London.

MILES GIBSON

The Sandman

PANTHER
Granada Publishing

Panther Books
Granada Publishing Ltd
8 Grafton Street, London W1X 3LA

Published by Panther Books 1985

First published in Great Britain by
William Heinemann Ltd 1984

ISBN 0-586-06084-7

Printed and bound in Great Britain by
Collins, Glasgow

Set in Baskerville

For Philippa

"Some say that gleams of a remoter world
visit the soul in sleep – that death is slumber."

Shelley

Chapter One

Tulip stood and stared at herself in the mirror. She was wearing a black satin dress, high-heeled mules and an absurd wig of thick treacle curls that fell, in glittering cascades, to her elbows. Beneath the wig her face seemed very small and flat. She had the eyes of a goldfish and a slightly crooked mouth. Her eyebrows were no more than tiny black brushstrokes and her lips a mere splash from a scarlet pen. She stared at herself and smiled. She was tired and bored. Her ankles ached from the cruel tilt of the mules. She cocked her head until a curtain of heavy curls obscured her view, parted the hair with her fingers, smiled again, thrust out her breasts, cradled her belly in plump white hands, flirted with herself in the glass. When she was satisfied with her reflection she turned her attentions upon the room.

The room was small and hot and filled by a clumsy old-fashioned bed. Beside the bed a red telephone and a large armchair. Behind the armchair a locked door. There was a wash-basin in one corner of the room. On a shelf above the basin a bowl crammed with tablets of scented soap. A glass vase of wilting flowers on a low metal table. Rugs on the floor. A blind of candy-coloured slats against the window. A bookshelf against one wall and a battered wardrobe. A collection of dolls on the bookshelf. Beside the wardrobe a second door that led to the stairs and the street.

Tulip walked to the bed and picked up a twisted pillow. She

punched it several times with her fist and threw it aside. She glanced at her watch. It was a little past ten-thirty and she had opened for business at noon. It had been a long and difficult day and it wasn't finished. She bent to the low metal table and plucked at one of the limp roses. The flower exploded between her fingers. She swore and searched for a cigarette, when the doorbell rang.

She walked to the door and drew back a chain. When she opened the door she found a young man in a heavy winter coat, clutching a leather bag in his hands, standing among the shadows. For some moments she stood and stared at him in silence. And then, with a little movement of her head, she beckoned him into her room.

"What shall I call you?" she asked as she turned to confront him.

"My name is William."

"That's nice. I'll call you Billy."

The man said nothing. He looked around the room. He was wearing a pair of heavy spectacles and he screwed up his eyes as he tried to peer through the smeared glass.

"Don't look so scared, Billy. I'm not going to eat you," chirruped Tulip. She began to laugh. She threw back her head and bared her teeth. But the man looked puzzled. When she saw that he was not amused she tried to compose herself, lit a cigarette, gave it several brief tugs and snorted smoke through her nose.

"Why don't you sit down, Billy, and take off your coat?"

The young man took off his coat and folded it carefully across the bed. He sat down in the armchair and placed the leather bag at his feet. His hair was short and shone like silver where it caught the light. He turned suddenly towards the door behind him and squinted at the keyhole, jerking his head as if listening for some faraway sound.

She took a step towards him, hesitated, glanced across his shoulder at the door. "That's my own private room, Billy," she said forcing another smile. "Would you like a drink?"

He frowned. "Is it empty?" he whispered.

"Yes, of course it's empty," she said with a laugh. "This is the room where I entertain. Don't worry, Billy, we're quite alone. Be brave and have a drink."

"Yes, thank you," he said.

"Scotch?"

"Fine."

She turned to a cabinet beside the bed. He was young and frightened. He looked as if he might faint if she touched him. Old men made difficult customers – they were always trying to smell your shoes or peer at your bum through a keyhole. They were unpredictable. But the young men, ah, they were quickly satisfied. They had no imagination. She stifled a yawn as she poured the Scotch. "I haven't seen you before," she said.

"No."

"Is this your first time?"

The young man nodded, adjusting the spectacles on his nose.

"That's nice," smiled Tulip. "Well, don't look so unhappy. You'll be fine. I've got clients who've been coming here for years and years. You'd be surprised. They're just like old friends. They look after me and I take care of them. You understand?"

The man nodded and sipped his Scotch. Tulip sat down on the edge of the bed and crossed her legs. A bracelet of silver beads sparkled on her ankle. She smiled and sucked at her cigarette. Through the shroud of smoke her eyes flickered across his face, his hands, his clothes, his shoes. Behind the greasy spectacles he had bright, green eyes. His hands were clean and dainty. She didn't like his hair.

"Some girls don't care," she complained. "They work the streets, steal your money while you're pressed against the wall with your pants around your knees. They give the business a bad name. I like to make my clients feel special. That's why I've gone to so much trouble here. It always pays to take a little extra trouble." She gestured around the room with a fat, white hand.

"I used to be a dancer," she explained, "I've had classical training. But I have very weak ankles. . ."

Without warning she opened the dress at her throat and

peeled it away from her shoulders and breasts. There was a pause in the undressing while she searched for an ashtray, picked it up, dropped it, damn, picked it up and stabbed it several times with her cigarette. Then she prised her fingers into the wrinkled satin that had bunched around her belly and pushed the dress to her knees. It fell whispering to her feet and she stepped out of it with a little wave of her hand and a smile.

She was wearing nothing but a pair of fine black stockings that cut wickedly into the tops of her thighs making the skin there seem excessively polished and fat. Her breasts were heavy and swung loosely when she moved. The nipples were small as buttons. She dipped her hand between her legs and tweaked at the hair between finger and thumb, twisting it into a long black curl. Then she lit another cigarette and perched on the arm of the chair, swinging her legs, rubbing a breast against the young man's face.

"There, Billy, isn't that nice?" she inquired. She pulled at the cigarette, threw back her head and blew smoke towards the ceiling.

Billy reached up and whispered into her ear, "I wonder if you would allow me to indulge in a little habit of mine?"

Tulip frowned and stood up. "What is it?" she asked suspiciously. "I don't want anything violent. And I don't do anything – you know – dirty. This is a nice place." She tugged in frustration at her cigarette and stared at his hair which had begun to glow with an unearthly light. It was bad enough having an old man peer at your bum through the keyhole without having a young one prancing around in bra and panties. She had hoped to attract a better class of customer.

"Oh, no, it's nothing unpleasant," said Billy soothingly. "But I'd feel much happier if I could wear my gloves."

She frowned and shrugged. It wasn't too bad. He might have wanted lipstick and a pair of high-heeled shoes.

"They seem to lend me so much confidence. I suppose it's the rubber. They have such a wonderful rubbery smell."

"Yeah, but what are you going to *do* with them?" she demanded darkly.

"Wear them," smiled Billy innocently. He drew a pair of gloves from the leather bag. A pair of rubber kitchen gloves.

"What else have you got in that bag?"

"Books," said Billy as he teased on the gloves.

"I read a book once," she said and crushed out her cigarette. Then the young man smiled again and opened his arms, inviting Tulip to embrace him. She stepped forward and he cradled the back of her skull in a fat rubber hand.

For a long time the man and the woman stood, wrapped together in a silent embrace. And then Tulip sank to her knees. The handle of a slender knife was stuck in her neck. A chrysanthemum of blood had blossomed brightly from her ear. The man staggered beneath the weight of the fallen woman, dragged her forward and allowed her to collapse in the chair.

When he had recovered his breath he stepped back a few paces to admire the corpse. She was sprawled, as if asleep, her arms hanging loose and her legs slightly parted. The stockings were wrinkled and torn loose from their moorings. Her head rested against one shoulder. She stared back at the man with her cloudy goldfish eyes.

He knelt down and tried to smooth the stockings against her knees but the gloves made him clumsy and he dragged down the stockings in exasperation, peeling them roughly from her toes. He stared up at the woman then and smiled blissfully. She wore the handle of the knife against her hair in the manner of a Japanese comb. The chrysanthemum had thickened and its petals were spreading against her neck. He stretched out and tenderly touched her face with his rubber fingertips. He closed her eyes and her mouth fell open. Her tongue was red as a pomegranate. He brushed the hair away from her breasts and arranged her hands in her lap. His touch was delicate and precise. She had lost her mules and he retrieved them, slipping them neatly onto her feet.

When he was satisfied with her appearance he took his leather bag from beneath the armchair and pulled out a Polaroid camera. He took three photographs of the woman and laid the prints along the edge of the bed where they ripened into glossy bruises. He peered at them anxiously, impatient to examine the portraits.

And then he thought he heard it. A scuffle, a muffled cough, a groan or a sigh. He didn't know – he couldn't say exactly what he heard – but he felt someone was watching him. He turned in horror towards the window and stared at the cracks in the metal blind. He swung towards the door and snarled. His hands were trembling. His face was yellow and glossy with sweat. There were eyes glinting from every shadow. High on the bookshelf the dolls' mouths hung open in silent screams. He twisted on his heel and scooped the pictures from the bed. He threw the pictures, the camera and tumbler of Scotch into the leather bag, bundled his coat beneath his arm and ran from the room into the cold and dangerous night.

Chapter Two

He woke up shouting and clutching the sheets. The room was in darkness. He rolled sideways and groped for the light, screwing up his face against the glare. Sleep had tortured his hair into damp brown spikes. His pyjamas were clinging and wet. He stumbled from the bed and stood shivering against the wall. For some moments he could not move but waited, listening for the sound of footsteps in the rooms beyond the door.

He wiped his face in his hands. He could hear nothing in the silence but the mad, clockwork chatter of his heart. He rubbed his hands against the wall and closed his eyes. In the darkness of his head he could see again the shape of the woman as she sank to her knees, the angle of the knife against her throat, the sudden rush of rubber and blood.

He shuffled to the far wall and peered through a chink in the dusty curtains. He could see no one waiting for him, no one beckoned or waved from the street. He turned away from the window and stared at the door. He was stupid with shock. His memory of the past few days was blurred, day and night smudged together so that he walked sometimes at midnight and slept at noon. He tried to concentrate, cut through the confusion and assemble the facts. Now he remembered the woman's name. Tulip. Her name was Tulip. He repeated the name several times, as if he was afraid he might lose it again. He remembered the heat of her skin and the curious glittering weight of her hair. What was she wearing? A dress, yes, a black dress and her legs were in stockings. There was a corset, a cobweb of pink rubber strands. No, that was another time. Another corpse. Dear God, so much blood.

His eyes hurt and his tongue felt swollen. He was haunted. The corpses followed him everywhere. When he slept he sensed them beside his bed, grinding their teeth as they watched him dream. When he went walking in the street he saw the dead among the living, a jostling crowd of corpses, staring at him as he hurried past.

He needed a cigarette. He tiptoed into the kitchen and found a crumpled pack of Camel. He smoothed the cigarette between finger and thumb but could not find his mouth. There were tears rolling from his eyes and dripping from the tip of his nose. He brushed at the tears with his fist and swore aloud. He must reach the telephone. He knew, at last, he must call the police. Yes, if there was time, if he could reach the phone before he was buried beneath the weight of the dead, he knew he'd be safe. He must surrender himself to the police.

The smoke burned his throat and clouded his head. Beneath the window of his study a small table and on the table a telephone. He moved towards it. The journey seemed endless, the floor expanding, the walls shrinking away from him. The light from the ceiling bleached his face as he passed beneath it. His shadow ballooned against the furniture, a black satin shroud sailing beside him. At last he reached the table and sank into the little chair beside the telephone. He stretched out his hand and then hesitated, his eyes drawn to a book almost hidden beneath the papers and half-forgotten letters. It was a cheap exercise book, grubby at the edges, the spine worn white, the pages filled black with tiny handwriting.

For a long time he sat and stared at the diary, his hand stretched out but the fingers withered and curled. He wanted to read it. He wanted to try and make sense of it again. The diary explained everything. He held it gently in his hands. The forbidden journal. The book of the dead. He turned the cover and began to read.

Chapter Three

THE JOURNAL

My name is William Mackerel Burton. I have killed eighteen men and women. It has been my life's work.

I am an artist. My work has been shown on television and acclaimed as a national scandal. The popular press has followed my career with feverish enthusiasm. My work has been reviewed in several languages. I am celebrated. A book has been published of my complete works. I have to confess, it is not a very good book – a lurid volume of bad photographs, rumours and gossip. A cheap paperback book of the dead. I bought a copy for my collection and discovered that many of the murders mentioned were quite unknown to me. They were counterfeits, clumsy copies in the style of the master. But I was flattered. I cannot complain. And this diary will, one day, correct their mistake.

I assume many shapes. I am Siva, purveyor of death in a thousand disguises. I am the Sandman. Doctor Death. The Golden Reaper. The nightmare of old ladies, the ambition of young men, the Hammersmith Horror, the Monster of Maida Vale, the London Butcher. But you, for reasons of personal comfort, may prefer to call me insane.

I am beyond capture. I shall retire and leave nothing behind but the silence. Can you imagine the sense of loss that overwhelms the artist at the prospect of leaving less than a thumbprint to mark his career? A painter hangs his daubs in public galleries, a sculptor plants his bronze in city parks and the people gather round to admire it. My work is also extraordinary and not without its beauty. Yet, once discovered, it is wrapped up in sheets and bundled away under cover of darkness. I do not beg your applause for the whisper of my knife or expect you to gawp at the blood of the corpse. But some account of my work is demanded.

Perhaps it would be easier, you suggest, to surrender myself and allow the authorities to broadcast the authorised version of my life? But what patience would they have for the explanations of a lunatic, a man who was asked the questions and invented his own replies? What do they understand of the artist and his vision? They trade in motives and morals, jealous husbands and greedy thieves. No, it is better that I explain myself in my own words.

How then shall I describe myself? I am the balance and the razor's edge. The snake in the grass. The grain of sand in the oyster's soft flesh. The shadow at the end of the street. The bogeyman beneath your bed. Others struggle to scrawl their likenesses on history's faded blackboard, repeating and repeating the same crude face. I am the man with the bright, wet sponge. I am the hand which wipes the board clean.

When I die I shall return to the world as a fatal disease for which there is no remedy. It will not be a painful or disfiguring disease. No, I've thought about it and I want to be an exotic fever. I will inhabit the bodies of young girls, heat them up until their breasts swell and their faces glow. I will appear suddenly and produce a strikingly beautiful corpse, so that people will say, if I must die, I hope I die of Mackerel Poisoning or Butcher's Brain or whatever they call me.

I am not without mercy for the mourners who fall on their knees behind me. But, you must understand, death is not a machine of my own invention. Death touches everyone. I merely choose the time and make the arrangements. My capture would not grant you eternal life. I would continue in the shape of a sudden chill, a faulty brake pedal, a spark of fire in the bedclothes. The evening news describes my arrest, you thank God for mercy, and the television explodes in your face. But I must make you understand. I must find the beginning and make you understand.

My mother kept a private hotel in a small, damp seaside town where the water was deep and the cliffs were as soft as cheese. All through the summer the house was crowded. There were strangers in every room. But during the winter the house was empty and the rooms smelt of paraffin and rain.

In those days I lived in the attic, a tiny kingdom of pygmy furniture and giant dolls. The walls were covered in a heavy yellow paper printed with rows of radishes. My kingdom contained a wardrobe, a table and a broken chair. I kept a bag of crayons on the table, a jigsaw puzzle of a flying boat and an alphabet book made from waterproof cardboard. The bed was a blue box with shallow wooden walls to prevent me from falling out of my dreams, over the floor and down the stairs. Beside the bed a tiny candle in a paper collar that glowed in the night for comfort. From the end of my bed I could sit and survey the dolls who kept sentry at the window.

The dolls were made from rags. They were nothing more than scarecrows sewn from petticoats and shirts, but I loved them. Sometimes, when I was alone, I would gather them together and lie beneath them while the herring gulls stared through the bars of the window.

There was one doll who became my favourite, a handsome creature with a cotton cushion for a head and glass button eyes. Her body was made from a satin blouse and although she was soft she felt especially heavy and warm. When I crawled beneath her on the bed I suffocated under her weight. For a time I refused to be parted from this shapeless concubine and often confused her with my mother.

My mother was a small woman with large red hands. She wore trousers and several cardigans. I cannot remember her face. During the first few years of my life I recognised her by the colour of her hands. And a very particular smell. Whenever I try to conjure up this early memory of my mother I can smell breakfast, for she had always cooked a dozen breakfasts before she came to wash and dress me and lead me down from the attic. Her embrace held the smoke of fried eggs and streaky bacon. If my mother came to haunt me now her ghost would hide in a trail of frying-pan smoke. For this reason I never eat breakfast. But then, in those faraway years, breakfast was the most glorious and exciting time of day.

The breakfast room was warm and filled by tables dressed in limp linen shrouds. I was too small to reach the tops of these tables so I crawled under them and sat in the twilight, sucking toastcrumbs I gleaned from the carpet and staring at the legs that surrounded me. Sometimes a hand would appear between a pair of knees and offer me a finger of toast soaked in egg yolk, a shred of bacon or a sugar lump. I crawled up and down the corridor of legs with my mouth open and my tongue hanging out.

After breakfast everyone left the house and I was taken to the kitchen and filled with rusks and milk until I was sick.

As I grew older the furniture in the attic shrank, holes appeared in the flying boat and geraniums replaced the radishes. The dolls turned shapeless and grey. My oldest friends began to rot and fall apart. One day I smuggled a pair of scissors into the attic and opened up my favourite, snipping at her dusty seams. I examined the contents of her stomach. I found a scrag-end of carpet, a small net curtain, a sock, a vest and sixpence. I buried the remains in a suitcase stored beneath the bed.

I was soon tall enough to rest my chin on the tops of breakfast tables and stare at the faces of strangers. I learned to stand motionless with my head balanced on the edge of the cloth, my mouth open, my eyes watching the movement of forks loaded with egg and bacon and sausage.

I was called Mackerel because for the first six or seven years of my life I never closed my mouth. I sucked air like a drowning fish. But it was not merely the promise of table scraps that made my jaw hang heavy in my face. Every time I saw a man or woman my mouth popped open in surprise. No matter how often I looked at them I never overcame my astonishment. At first they were only hands, legs and sandals leaking sand. As I grew older and taller their faces came into view and the shock was too much for me. I had expected the same, simple pastry cut-out that I saw whenever I looked at myself in the mirror.

Sultana eyes and a keyhole mouth. Instead, these faces were huge and bruised and forlorn. There were long, wrinkled faces the colour of rotting apples. There were broad, scarlet faces with the skin falling off in silver flakes. There were swollen faces that blistered and bubbled and shone.

One night, as my mother helped me into bed, I described these various skin complaints. She shrugged her shoulders and told me that people liked to sit in the sun. But I knew she was trying to conceal the truth. Sometimes she smeared a gobbet of calamine on my nose, forced a hat down over my ears and sat *me* in the sun. I remained as pale as distemper. These people were not sitting in the sun. These people were falling apart and had probably come here to die. I had seen it happen to my dolls. I rolled another question around my mouth but my mother was too quick for me, pressed a finger against my lips and clucked impatiently.

"Shut up, Mackerel. Close your eyes or the Sandman will catch you."

"Who?" I demanded with interest.

"The Sandman. He's a wicked old man who catches children when they won't go to sleep and sprinkles sand in their eyes."

"Does he live on the beach?"

"No, he tiptoes around peeping through bedroom windows searching for children who won't close their eyes."

"Why?"

"You can ask him yourself when he taps on the glass," she sighed and snapped out the light.

Well, it was a complete mystery. I imagined the Sandman as a local barbarian, half man and half beast, a shambling corpse packed full of wet sand. I never saw him while awake but I often saw him when asleep. As I grew older my dreams grew darker.

My new growth also gave me a better view of my mother. I discovered that her face was plump as an egg and speckled with tiny freckles. Her hair was the colour of a certain inferior brand of toffee and she wore metal rings in her ears. Her mouth looked very small and her eyebrows were drawn with a pencil. I liked to sit on her lap and stare at the face, tracing its lines with my finger. The breakfast fumes in her cardigans were forgotten at such a height as I nuzzled my nose against her skin, searching for the little patch of Yardley scent she liked to keep on her neck.

It was about this time that Uncle Eno first noticed me under his feet. He was a tall, narrow man who smelt of tobacco and Brilliantine. He wore sunglasses and a green shirt. He did not leave after breakfast and sit in the sun with the other guests, but seemed to walk around the house for hours and stare through the windows in silence. There was an expression of unspeakable sadness about him. Whenever he caught sight of me he would bend down slowly, pat my head in a friendly manner and breathe over me. His breath was as black as funerals.

He came to the house each August and slept in the bedroom under my attic. I was always excited when his enormous leather suitcase appeared in the hall. He was a mysterious figure and I fancied he came to shelter with us from some great personal tragedy. I suspected a tragedy because my mother cooked him special breakfasts which he shared with me in the kitchen. He was my mother's favourite and I could understand her feelings – my own favourite having only recently been laid to rest. My mother suffered regular bad health throughout the month of August and she often told me that Uncle Eno proved a comfort.

"Your Uncle Eno has come as a blessing," she would declare as she loaded his plate with bacon, "He's a great comfort to your poor mother."

"You're a fine woman," Uncle Eno would say as he waved his fork in her face. "And you shouldn't be ashamed of your appetites."

My mother cast an anxious glance in my direction. Good grief. I had never seen my mother's appetites, but I hoped they were not infectious – I certainly didn't want them.

Uncle Eno was especially sympathetic to her complaints, I concluded, because he suffered some rare and malignant disease of his own. Sometimes, on quiet afternoons when the house was empty and nothing could be heard but the faint echo of gulls in the chimneys, my mother would collapse on a sofa and complain of a tightness in her stomach. Then Uncle Eno would sit beside her, stroke one of her big red hands and make soothing noises in his throat. The tightness must have been very uncomfortable because finally Uncle Eno would have to unbuckle her trousers and rub her stomach to ease the pain. My mother would moan as he rubbed the affected parts but it did not frighten me. I knew, of course, she was having more trouble with her appetites. But on the few occasions I tried to catch sight of them Uncle Eno would winkle me out of my hiding place and send me away to buy chocolate.

I was a happy child. The days passed blissfully. I sang and danced and blew bubbles of chocolate over my chin. I stared at the world and laughed.

Does the knowledge upset you? Would you prefer that Mackerel the murderer, the London Butcher, had been shackled in the cellar and beaten with a leather strap? Would it suit your sensibilities to learn that I had been locked in a cage, neglected, deprived and deserted by my mother? Would it help you make sense of my life? Would your sleep be sweetened by the knowledge that my brains had been poisoned in childhood? It seems a shame to disappoint you but, alas, my early years were happy as a picture book.

There were long, parched afternoons when I was marooned on the beach and made to pick sand from packets of tomato sandwiches. There were nights of tremendous blustering storms when the streets sparkled with salt and the sea coughed seaweed against the windows. There were bonfires big as haystacks and fireworks that fell in the mud and shot sparks into my hair and eyelashes. There were Christmas parties when the house was lost in a fog of blue cigar smoke and the carpets were sharp with pine needles. There were birthday parties when I dribbled warm sugar over my wrists and glued my hands to the curtains. There were conjuring tricks and clockwork boats, tin trumpets and goldfish. There were rubber cushions that farted, magnets, footballs and invisible ink. I was deprived of nothing. I was gorged on the richest foods and wrapped in the warmest overcoats. My mother and father did everything they could to entertain and amuse me. I have none but tender memories of them.

Although the first time I remember taking any particular notice of my father was the day I found his corpse on the kitchen floor.

It was November and the house was empty. My throat was sore and I had been kept away from school for a week. Boys who breathed through their mouths, my mother warned, were prone to sore throats. I shuffled aimlessly through the house, wrapped in a dressing-gown and scarf. It was three o'clock in the afternoon and nearly dark. My mother was asleep in her room.

I was passing the kitchen door when I was suddenly seized with a craving for biscuits. The biscuits responsible for my addiction were called Godfrey's Fingers. They were long, brittle sticks dusted on one side with grains of sugar that flashed like a coat of mashed glass. The thought of them made me sweat with lust. I stood trembling by the kitchen door, coiling the scarf around my chin and mouth and plotting their theft. My mother, who was never sympathetic to the weaknesses of the addict, kept Godfrey's Fingers in a tin box on the highest and most difficult shelf in the kitchen. It needed a crafty eye and a lot of courage to recover them. But the addict Mackerel had a measure of both when the lust was upon him.

The kitchen was full of shadows. I crept through a crack in the door and tiptoed towards the great chest of drawers that guarded the larder. I had learned from experience to pull open each of the drawers (baking tins, ladles, knives and roasting trays), until they formed a rickety ladder over which I could scramble and scratch my way to the top. And there, among the cobwebs and earwigs, on the very roof of the chest, lay the magic box of Fingers. It was a dangerous climb for a small boy and made Godfrey's holy digits taste even spicier.

The box, when I reached it, opened with a startled gasp. I tucked five fingers into the pocket of my dressing-gown and turned to make the descent. It was my second robbery of the week and, despite my sore throat, I loved to break the biscuits into pieces and let them dissolve slowly against the roof of my mouth until there was nothing left except the buttery sweetness. Their delicate flavour–and the length of time it took me to suck each biscuit into nothing–usually drove me into the lavatory where I knew I could enjoy myself without being disturbed.

I had reached the ground, my scarf full of spiders and my mouth full of biscuit, when I noticed my father. He was spread on the floor beneath the far window. Had he been there all the time, I wondered, or had he tiptoed through the door while my attention had been taken up with the biscuit box and I was safely out of view beneath the ceiling.

It was a surprise to see my father in the house at that time in the afternoon. During the winter he took a job with the council, painting the promenade railings, and he did not usually come home until I was in bed and asleep. Why then had he appeared so abruptly on the kitchen floor?

While I was wrestling with this problem it dawned on me that he was flat on his back. It was perfectly natural, as far as I was concerned, to jump or roll or scamper about on my hands and knees. But I had never seen men or women attempt any of these more eccentric forms of locomotion. And, anyway, he was not moving but simply lay there on his back, arms folded neatly over his stomach, and stared at the ceiling.

I coughed at him. It hurt my throat but he did not turn his head in my direction. I grunted at him. I whistled and clapped my hands. But my father continued to ignore me.

After a few minutes in which neither of us moved I shuffled across the kitchen to take a closer look at him. His face was a most unusual colour. The skin was a sinister shade of slush and his eyes were yellow. I waggled my hands in his face and stuck out my tongue. But nothing seemed to draw his attention.

I could not understand it. I sat down beside him and waited for him to recognise me. It was dark and cold on the kitchen floor. I turned, for comfort, to Godfrey's Fingers. I recovered one of them from my dressing-gown pocket and pushed it firmly between my father's teeth. It stuck out of his mouth like the handle of a swordswallower's blade. He made no attempt to suck or chew this precious offering. It was a waste.

Finally I grew tired of watching him and retired to the lavatory to suck my remaining Fingers. I cannot remember when my mother discovered the corpse or what happened to me during the following hours. But by the next morning it was obvious that some kind of holiday had been declared and I was delivered into the hands of a distant aunt.

I understood that my father had died but it did not trouble me. He had gone but, I felt certain, one day he would come back. Everyone else came back to us in the season. For a little while I missed him. I continued to look for him when the doorbell rang or someone moved on the stairs, but then I forgot. My father had died. I accepted it. My aunt informed me he had gone to Heaven but I preferred to believe he had gone to Bolivia. Why he had lain down on the kitchen floor and refused to speak to me before his departure was a mystery.

The aunt owned a large apartment in a crumbling Victorian mansion on the seafront of a neighbouring town. My room was huge and cold and draughty. The windows rattled behind their curtains and the bed creaked when I moved my head. I hated it. I hated the heavy furniture cut from slabs of purple wood, the threadbare carpet and the gloomy etchings on the wall. In protest I cried myself to sleep each night which seemed to satisfy my aunt who thought the tears were dedicated to my father. She would creep to my bedside in the dark and dry my face by pressing it into the folds of her dress. Her body was hot and smelt of talcum powder. I learned to cry loudly and to great effect.

It was during this strange holiday that I met Dorothy. She was the daughter of the local grocer but seemed to prefer the company of my aunt for she spent every afternoon in the house. She was a few years older than myself and built like a greyhound. My aunt told her to treat me kindly because I had recently discovered my father's corpse and was suffering from the shock. My aunt confessed this in a loud whisper, shielding her mouth from me with the back of her hand, as if I had caught my father walking around in my mother's underwear and I would soon need my brains examined. Dorothy was fascinated.

The next afternoon she arrived with a loaf of stale bread tucked under her arm. She stood and stared at me for some time and then invited me to walk with her to feed the gulls on the beach. I was flattered.

The sea lay very quiet, a molten depth of grey marble beneath a wrinkled skin. When the skin was stretched the heavy veins rolled translucent in the sun. She faced the sea, screwing up her face against the glare, holding out the loaf and tearing at its crust. She threw a morsel of the bread high into the air where a gull snatched it with a greedy swoop. Then, to my amazement, the sky was full of gulls, wheeling and screaming above our heads. Dorothy broke the loaf into pieces, laughing and tossing them into the sky. The birds swarmed above her, grey rags in the silver light. When the bread was finished she brushed her hands clean of crumbs and stared at me thoughtfully.

"What did it look like when you found it?" she asked at last.

"What?"

"The corpse," she said eagerly.

I shrugged. I couldn't remember anything remarkable about it.

"It was on the floor," I said casually.

"Did it have its eyes open?" she asked as she pulled off her shoes.

I nodded.

"Did you close them?"

I shook my head.

"Did you cover it with a sheet?" she asked breathlessly.

"No."

"Weren't you frightened?" she demanded impatiently.

"No," I said, "I gave it a biscuit."

She shrieked, threw away her shoes and ran into the sea.

The water swilled around her calves. Her skin glittered with salt. The edges of her skirt were wet.

I walked at a distance from the water, holding her shoes in my hand. I held them carefully, letting them dangle by their straps and watched her balance in the waves.

The wind, scudding at an angle across the water, caught beneath her skirt and lifted it briefly, exposing the backs of her thighs. I called out to her and she turned to face me. Her hair flew into her eyes. She waved and tried to run through the waves towards me, her legs kicking and plunging through the grey foam.

She was cold and shivering when she returned. Her feet were caked with sand and she tried to smack them clean with her hands, leaning on me for support.

"When I die, I shall have hundreds of candles," she said.

"When are you going to die?" I asked her with considerable interest.

"Oh, I haven't made up my mind," she sighed and her tone of voice suggested that it might happen at any moment.

We walked home holding hands and I made her promise that if she decided to die while I stayed with my aunt she would come and die in my room.

Her interest in corpses inspired Dorothy to devise a game which we played in secret whenever my aunt went to visit my mother. Dorothy was always left to guard me on these occasions and we could run wild in the apartment for hours. The game would begin with Dorothy demanding a full description of my father. I was already bored with the story but recited it patiently while she sat on the floor and squirmed. When she was satisfied that I had omitted nothing we could play the game. I was made to lie on the carpet with my eyes closed and assume the role of the corpse while she, dancing on tiptoe around me, had to bring me back from the dead. She tried to work this miracle by a dozen ingenious tortures, each one inflicted upon me suddenly and without warning. She tickled the soles of my feet with a spoon, spat on my face and poked pencils in my ears. I resisted bravely but always came alive again, shouting and spluttering and calling her a cheat.

When I was restored to life it was Dorothy who became the corpse. She seemed to prefer this part of the game for she swore and snorted impatiently if I remained dead for more than five minutes. She would take off her dress, to save creasing it, and throw herself down dressed in nothing but her blue cotton knickers. The sight of her sprawled on the floor at my feet, with her eyes closed and her long greyhound legs thrown apart, gave me a strange feeling of warm wax melting and moving in my stomach. I stared at her without daring to shake her awake. Her sharp knees developed a faint blue blush from the draughts. Her nipples darkened and grew by some diabolical magic I did not understand. I would squat beside her and peer at the body with a delicious blend of horror and delight while the warm wax burned inside me.

I usually managed to break through the trance and inflict a number of small cruelties on her arms and legs. But nothing I devised could bring her back from the dead. She lay there with her eyes screwed shut, her breath reduced to short, panting rasps, and refused to be saved. Finally I would grow bored and wander away. The wax cooled and hardened. I forgot about her and left the room. Then she would throw a tantrum, chase me up and down the stairs and demand that the game begin again.

One afternoon, when I was bruised and bored by being dragged back from death by Dorothy, she invented a variation of the game in an attempt to revive my interest. The corpse, she whispered dramatically, would go and hide somewhere in the apartment and need to be hunted before it could be trapped and brought back to life. I had reservations about this graveyard hide-and-seek but Dorothy was thrilled by the notion and volunteered to be the first to creep away and die.

I stood in the parlour with my hands over my face and counted slowly and loudly to fifty. The silence, when I had finished my count, was formidable. I bravely trotted from room to room, poking under tables and reaching behind cupboards, but the corpse had vanished.

It was several anxious minutes before I discovered the first clue to Dorothy's chosen burial ground. Her dress was hanging limply from my aunt's bedroom door. I sneaked into the bedroom and dropped onto my hands and knees, scampering across the carpet to peer under the bed. But the room was empty. The great feather mattress lay undisturbed. The black Victorian dressing-table had not been touched. The long velvet curtains concealed nothing but dust. I looked around nervously. My aunt's bedroom had always been closed to me. I retreated to the safety of the door when I saw the second clue in front of the wardrobe.

Now the wardrobe was especially fearsome, the size of a gothic chapel, the whole decorated with carved wooden monkeys and oak leaves and vines, it stood on massive panther feet and cast a giant shadow across the room. The door of the wardrobe held a mottled, oblong mirror and reflected in the mirror I caught sight of a pair of blue cotton knickers crumpled in a heap on the carpet. The wardrobe had obviously eaten Dorothy.

I shuffled towards it and prised back the great door, inch by groaning inch. There, made blue by the gloom of coats and dresses, lay the naked greyhound, slumped in a corner with her arms wrapped over her head. She had died in such a manner that very little of the corpse was available to my inquisitive fingers. I stepped into the creaking tomb and allowed the door to swing shut behind me.

Wedging myself in the opposite corner I stretched out my arms through the shifting screens of silk and fur until I had grasped as much as I could of the rigid Dorothy. I groped and strained until I was in full possession of her leg. It was only one of her legs, true, but it was complete from the sharp blade of the ankle to the heat of her hip. I needed both hands to hold it steady, to stop it shrugging free and shrinking back again into the darkness. The only weapon available was my tongue. I flicked it out and ran it experimentally along the edge of her knee. The skin was rough but she gave a little shudder that encouraged me. And so, hidden in the mothballed darkness, beneath the rustling of my aunt's frocks, kneeling on a leather handbag, I began to lick the leg into life. It was a great success.

Dorothy, much to my surprise, began to whimper, softly at first, but then long and loudly. Encouraged by her protests, and seeking softer pastures for my grazed mouth, I moved higher, darting and dribbling over the brow of her hip. She thrashed around and tried to kick out but I held onto the leg and fought to pull it harder against me. She twisted suddenly and fell on her back so that my head was catapulted forward into her lap. My mouth was filled for a moment with unexpected beard. I was electrified. My tongue curled up in fright.

Dorothy moaned horribly, as if she were about to die for a second time, and fled into the daylight. I scrambled after her, frightened by the noises she made and trying to nurse my tongue in my hand. By the time I had gathered my wits the corpse had pulled itself back into its clothes and was busy trying to tidy the wardrobe.

She did not, as I feared, appear angry or hurt. Instead, she made me swear to tell no one of our game and then, in the same breath, made me promise to play it again the next day. I nodded and sucked my tongue in silence. I had a lot to think about. But we never played the game again. My aunt returned that afternoon and told me I was going home. My relief at escaping from the antics of the wild and snapping greyhound was mixed with a peculiar sense of disappointment.

When I returned to the hotel late the next morning I found that my father was still reported missing in Bolivia and Uncle Eno was sitting at the kitchen table nursing a mug of Bovril. As soon as he saw me he fished in his pocket for chocolate but my mother swept me into her arms and carried me to the attic. She looked very old. I studied her carefully while she helped me unpack my little cardboard suitcase. She was dressed, I noticed, in a new black cardigan and my father's best trousers. Her freckles had turned as grey as pepper and her nostrils were raw and peeling. Her eyes, when she returned my concentrated stare, were milky as glass buttons. She reminded me of my rag doll harem in the last hours of its decay.

Uncle Eno did everything he could to charm and please the

poor woman. He offered her bottles of Guinness and little bars of Yardley soap wrapped in cellophane. I did not see him rub her belly again but he often patted her baggy trousered bottom in a comforting manner. I was happy that he tried to help but, on one occasion, however, he went too far and shocked me. I distinctly saw him pull out his pocket handkerchief and allow my mother to blow her nose in it. To my horror she gave several wet snorts, bunched up the sodden rag and stuffed it back into Uncle Eno's jacket pocket. I could hardly believe my own eyes. It was the most disgusting act I had ever witnessed and made me shiver for a week at the memory of it.

But despite the kind attentions of Uncle Eno, my mother's health did not improve and her pains seemed too deep now to be penetrated by his supple fingers. The evening of his departure he bent his big, sad face against mine and breathed over me. His melancholy seemed to have navigated new depths of despair. For some minutes he could not even speak but merely wagged his head from side to side forlornly.

"You're a queer fish, young Mackerel," he said at last.

"Yes, uncle."

He wagged his head again and sucked on a tooth. "I want you to take some advice."

"Yes, uncle."

"Never trust anyone – take my advice – never trust anyone and you'll live to be ninety. Do I make myself understood?"

"Yes, uncle."

He ruffled my hair with his hand and smiled sadly. "You must look after your mother for me, Mackerel," he said in farewell. "Remember, you're the man of the house."

I was not impressed with my promotion to the adult world. My opinion of men and women had not improved with my father's death.

The new man of the house stood in the bathroom and watched the blood flow down his neck. He was bleeding from both nostrils, fat scarlet worms that moved warmly against his chin and were creeping gradually towards his chest. A young man who breathed through his mouth, my mother warned, was prone to bleed from the nose. She did not offer any explanation. She had made it sound like some peculiar ritual the body must perform to turn the boy into man. For this reason I felt as proud and frightened as a ripe girl at the sight of her own blood. The second flow in a week. I watched the blood shine in the mirror and wondered if I would bleed to death. But the worms stopped moving, wrinkled darkly and failed to make their escape. I splashed water over the worms, hoping to revive them, watching them melt and stain my skin.

I was sixteen years old. The face that stared back at me from the mirror was neither ugly nor handsome. The eyes that admired the blood stains on my chin were neither kindly nor cruel: they were green. The nose was straight, the mouth full and hanging open. The teeth were slightly crooked. The hair was limp and badly cut around the ears. I had freckles and a moustache too soft to shave. It was an ordinary face that could be seen once and immediately forgotten. I helped my mother in the hotel and no one raised an eyebrow in admiration or disgust. No one noticed when I passed through a door or stood behind their chair. It was an ordinary face. The perfect face of murder. I cannot remember the ambitions that clawed impatiently between the ears of this pale young man. He worked hard and said nothing. Life presented itself as a long, straight and virtually deserted street along which he expected to stroll at a slow and dignified pace. He rarely laughed, yet, equally, he rarely woke in the night and screamed. He was polite to guests and clean in his habits. He had an altogether mild and gentle temperament. The perfect temper for murder.

The worms were dead. I tried several brisk snorts to open my nostrils but they were firmly plugged with blood. Reluctantly I had to declare the bleeding complete and continue with the morning's work. My duties began at dawn and rarely finished until midnight. My mother needed help to crack eggs, toast bread and open marmalade. I served at the tables, swept the floors, scrubbed the kitchen and fed the boiler. I balanced the books, weighed the laundry and measured the sugar into the bowls.

A girl arrived late in the morning to make the beds and wash the dishes. Her name was Wendy Figg. She was the size of a sofa and had a dainty Victorian porcelain face on which she liked to paint expressions of innocent surprise. Her eyebrows were drawn into arches and her cheeks were flushed. Her mouth was puckered as if she was nursing a grape between her lips and her teeth. She rarely painted her lips but they were always red. She kept her hair in neat yellow bunches, tied with ribbons. This prim and dainty effect was made spectacular by the rest of her body which had all the broad, slack, comfortable qualities of parlour furniture. She liked to dress in frocks cut from heavy velvet that reminded me of cushion covers, but when she worked she favoured a thin nylon coat through which I could see the struggle of her underwear. Her hands were pale and fat and she wore an engagement ring on one spiky finger. A little cauliflower of diamond grit and glass.

My favourite duty of the day was watching Figg make the beds. My mother did not trust Figg to work alone in the rooms and insisted that I follow her from bed to bed and discourage her from stealing the soap. My mother, bad health forbidding her to work at anything but the lightest tasks as I grew old enough to manage the heaviest , had taken out a subscription to a romantic book club. Her brains were quickly addled with tales of fainting virgins, brutal pirates and servants who peered through keyholes and stole family fortunes. Poor Figg was my mother's idea of a servant. She was convinced that the girl's pockets were crammed with slivers of soap. Every Sunday I was sent upstairs to count the soap and record my findings in a small notebook. I did nothing to defend Figg's honesty. Watching her work gave me so much pleasure that I did not want to lose my excuse for squatting in corners and trying to squint up her skirts. I don't believe Figg ever knew of my mother's mad suspicions and, anyway, she seemed glad of my company.

I dried my chin on the edge of a towel and joined Figg in the bedroom.

"Have you stopped bleeding, Mr Burton?" she asked over

her shoulder. I liked the way she called me Mr Burton. It was foolish. Perhaps, after all, my mother was correct and Figg was a natural servant.

"Yes, thank you," I said and sat down beneath the window. Figg was bending over the bed, chopping at the sheets with her hands to smooth out the wrinkles. The front of her coat fell open and I feasted for a moment on the heaving shadows.

"It looked horrible," she said happily.

"You can die from a nose bleed," I said darkly.

"It would take a long time," she laughed and gave the mattress a friendly slap. Her engagement ring sparkled in the dust.

"Is Percy coming to meet you today?" I asked her casually. Figg nodded and blushed. She dragged a blanket into place and then tucked it vigorously in.

I loved to make Figg blush. I hated Percy. He was the man who had bought her the ring and he usually loitered outside in the street, whistling and picking his nose, until Figg had finished her work. There was no doubt that they loved each other but the sight of them together made me jealous. Figg dropped the pillow and stooped to retrieve it. A button fell from her coat and rolled under the bed. I peeped into her shadows again and saw they had cleared to reveal a big breast nesting in a stiff cotton cup. I swallowed hard and found myself blushing. Figg swung the pillow onto the bed and tweaked its corners with her fingers.

"Will you get married?" I asked.

Figg sat down on the edge of the mattress and sighed. It was the last bed of the day and she was tired.

"Yes, I think we'll get married."

"When?" I could not resist asking the question although I dreaded the answer. I knew that as soon as Percy managed to marry my Figg she would no longer be allowed to come and work at the hotel. Percy would forbid it. I hated the prospect of losing her morning visit. I wanted nothing to change. I wanted to be able to walk around an eternity of little bedrooms, peeping between the buttons of Figg's nylon coat and gloating at her underwear.

"Perhaps in the autumn, if we can afford it. Or perhaps we'll wait until the spring," she said at last.

"You might get tired of him," I suggested hopefully and smiled balefully at her knees.

"What d'you mean?" she said.

"Well, you might find someone else. A millionaire, a film star," I conjectured lamely.

"But I love Percy," she protested.

"Yes, but you *might* meet someone else. You must not be impatient. You shouldn't throw yourself away," I warned.

"I'm not throwing myself away, Mr Burton," said Figg, a trifle annoyed.

"But you could marry anybody in the world," I laughed bitterly.

"Ah, but there's no one quite like Percy," she said and carefully crossed her legs.

Her voice softened whenever she spoke about Percy. It was the tone of voice old women use on their poodles. And her expression widened from surprise into amazement. She perched on the end of the bed and stared in silence at the wall. I was wounded.

"You've lost a button," I snorted and marched from the room.

I skulked behind the curtains in the breakfast room, watching Percy strutting up and down the street, until the front door slammed and Wendy Figg ran to join him. I saw him grin and lock his arm around her neck. She said something in his ear which made him glance back in my direction and sneer. Then they walked away.

What made Percy so attractive to women? He was a monster. His hair was long and oiled. His mouth was full of broken teeth. I couldn't understand it. He was nothing but a villain in a cheap suit and elasticated boots.

I spent the rest of the day on my hands and knees, scrubbing the kitchen floor and dreaming of Figg's breast bulging from its cotton sling. I had made no real friends at school and the hotel prevented me from finding adventure on the beach where a thousand office girls buttered and burned themselves in the sun. Figg's fat breast was my singular object of desire. It haunted and tickled and teased me until I had worked the floor into a stupendous lather. My ears burned. My hands trembled. While I tried to rinse my scrubbing brush in the bucket my elbow clipped the draining board and knocked a milk jug on to the floor.

It landed badly and exploded loud enough to wake my mother from her latest romantic adventure. She came limping into the kitchen, clucking and flapping her wrists.

"What will you do when I'm gone?" she chided as she helped me to pick up the pieces.

"Gone?"

"I won't last forever," she threatened, wiping her hands on her cardigan.

"I don't know. . ." I shook my head.

"Well, you can't come with me. You'll have to stay here," she said, as if she already knew that the Kingdom of Heaven would refuse me entry.

"Alone?" I was suddenly shocked by the idea.

"Good gracious! You'll get married – the hotel will belong to you," she said to comfort me.

"So nothing will change," I suggested.

"It will please your father. . ." she whispered and patted my hand.

I said nothing. Sometimes she grew confused and spoke about my father as if he were not dead but merely gone on a long journey. There were moments when I wondered again if he was really still alive and hiding in some Bolivian mining camp, writing my mother secret letters on onion skin paper which she hid beneath her bed. But, gradually, as her condition grew worse, my mother would begin to talk about my father as if he were sitting in the next room and it was she who had died and was reaching out to him from another world. When this notion invaded her brain she refused to eat and crept around the house dressed in a blanket. I did my best to keep her hidden under the stairs because I was anxious she should not frighten the guests.

That night I woke up to find my pillow sodden with blood. My mother remained calm as she helped me change the linen.

But I knew there was something wrong and the next day the doctor was summoned and shone a torch up my nose. I spent my birthday in a hospital bed with my nose wrapped in a bandage.

No one told me why they thought it necessary for a surgeon to poke needles into my nostrils. I knew that if I asked my mother what was happening she would shrug and call it the penalty paid by those who breathe through the mouth. But I accepted the treatment with few complaints, sat in my pyjamas and peered at people along a gun barrel of gauze bandage. The summer season had almost finished and I felt confident that my mother, with Figg's assistance, could manage very well without me. Her health seemed to improve when I was not there to nurse it. I was content to sit in my hospital bed and spit into freckled enamel bowls.

They knocked me out and worked on my nose as soon as I arrived and my first full view of the ward was painful and slightly blurred at the edges. I discovered an old man grinning at me from the adjacent bed. He was a collection of yellow bones sewn roughly together at the joints and pasted over with skin. He breathed with a whistle and smelt like a horse.

"Are you going to die?" he whispered gleefully.

I shook my head carefully. The question had taken me by surprise and I needed time to consider the prospect.

"It happens to everyone," he insisted. "Your tongue goes black and your lungs collapse. Your toes shrivel and your fingers drop off. They tie a knot in your rhubarb and stare at you. After a while they throw you away – dig a big hole and drop you in it. I know, it happened to a friend of mine once." He cackled and wheezed with delight as he remembered it. The next morning the bed was empty.

At breakfast they gave me a bowl of grey porridge. The handle of the spoon stuck out from its centre like the arm of a man drowned in glue. I felt lonely and confused. But the other patients in the ward introduced themselves and soon accepted me as a member of their tribe. They shuffled around the bed, pulling open their pyjamas, prodding at their bandages and offering me snorts of smuggled rum or special prices on black market cigarettes.

The empty bed was filled, a few days later, by a man called Blakey. He was a plumber with a blockage in one of his pipes. He was a plumber during the day but at night he became a magician. It was his passion and his pride.

Blakey was the man who changed my life. He made no deliberate attempt to influence me in argument or discussion. But he had a profound effect upon my feeble imagination which he nourished and exercised until it had a life of its own. It was magic. Blakey could snap his fingers and turn the world upside down. He could turn milk into water and hospital sheets into flags of all nations. He could steal the buttons from your pyjamas and pluck hens' eggs from the ears of exasperated nurses.

He was a large man with the complexion of a peeled grape. An ugly, steaming bulk of a man. Yet although he looked massively clumsy he had the most dainty hands which he liked to display by keeping them folded against his chest. They curled from the sleeves of his dressing-gown like a pair of pale and venomous snakes, waiting to dart at the unsuspecting spectator. They moved so fast that they left you breathless, wondering what trick they had performed while you were blinking. When he slept he left his upper teeth in a tumbler of water beside his bed and even this seemed to be some diabolical magic designed to intimidate me.

Blakey introduced himself by snatching a green silk chrysanthemum from thin air, offering it to me with a flourish and then making it explode into blue confetti as I reached towards it. This caused a great burst of applause in the ward and a withering scowl from the matron. I was enchanted.

At first he refused to discuss his conjuring tricks when I asked to know their secret.

"Magic is the art of the impossible," he would declare.

"Show me," I demanded.

"A magician never reveals his tricks. It's against the law," he said majestically.

"I won't tell anyone. I promise," I said. But Blakey would only tap his nose mysteriously and smile.

As time passed, however, he grew easier to hold in conversation and taught me to juggle bananas and throw my voice.

"A great magician can do anything. He can even make himself disappear," he revealed one morning.

"Can you disappear?" I inquired.

"Yes, if I say the magic words."

"Whisper them in my ear," I begged.

"No, I can't even whisper them," he said. "If I whispered the magic words in your ear we'd both disappear."

Blakey taught me that it was possible to control and contradict the natural order of the world. He taught me that laws were made to be broken and that, in breaking them, it is necessary to know of other, secret laws. He taught me that any attempt to solve a mystery is doomed to failure because it merely creates new mysteries that have no solution. Blakey taught me all these things without the need to talk of any of them. He snapped his fingers and produced a shower of snowflakes, a peach, a pencil or a puppet made from bandages.

Here was power beyond my understanding. Power that might make me master of the known world. I juggled my bananas with greater concentration. I must make my fingers dance. I must touch without touching. I would practise until I could plop one of Figg's fat breasts into the palm of my hand without her knowledge. I tried to throw my voice across greater distances. I wanted to be able to answer for my father when my mother, in her mad moments, tried to call to him through closed doors. I would learn to breathe fire, swallow razor blades and cut beautiful women in half. Who could resist such magic?

My mother came to visit me only twice during my time in hospital. On her first visit, the evening after my operation, she brought magazines and Lucozade, biscuits and plums. She was full of laughter and nonsense, clucking sympathetically at my wounded nose and resisting her usual temptation to tell me to shut my mouth. She charmed everyone in the ward.

They grinned foolishly from the beds and tried to comb their hair with their fingers. I was very proud and reached out to kiss her as she left but only succeeded in bending my bandage.

Her second visit, the day before my release, was a very different affair. I did not recognise her when she first appeared at the door. She had withered into her cardigans and her face was grey. I had been waiting for her impatiently, anticipating the general admiration of the ward and hoping to demonstrate my new skills as a magician. But the moment she sat down in the chair beside my bed I knew she was lost. Her feet had found their way to the hospital but her mind was far away. She sat in silence for some minutes and when she finally spoke it was in a crushed whisper, her face tilted towards my pillow.

She had come to complain about my father. He refused to help her manage the hotel, would not lift a finger in the kitchen and sulked all day in his room. The butcher sold her condemned beef, the servants stole the soap and my father did nothing but sit in his room and whistle. I listened to her with dismay and wondered how poor Figg could survive with this mournful old lunatic bickering at her heels. My mother had often brought my father back from the dead but this time she seemed determined not to let him slip away again.

I held her hand and let her whisper her complaints to my pillow. I did not relish the prospect of going home.

The following morning I said goodbye to Blakey and was released from hospital before breakfast. My mother seemed pleased to see me home again and fed me a quart of chicken soup. The last guest had left the hotel and the town was closed for the winter. Storms rolled off the Atlantic and scrubbed the streets. I rested, practised my conjuring tricks and watched the rain chatter against the windows.

My mother had no more complaints against my father and her recovery seemed as shocking to me as her madness. The ancient bundle of misery that had sat beside my hospital bed bloomed again within a few days until she looked absurdly young. She curled her hair and painted her fingernails. She did not abandon her cardigans but their colours grew brighter, she even wore bracelets and a smudge of rouge. Perhaps I felt uneasy with this relaxed and happy woman, for I kept expecting her to crumple once more into madness. But she gave no sign of trying to bring back my father, and he, for his part, did not seem anxious to return.

We worked together through that winter, varnished the stairs, painted the bedrooms and boiled the curtains.

During the long evenings I tried to entertain her with my modest magic, making her hoot and clap her hands as I fumbled with scarves and playing cards. For a few cold months we were happy together.

My mother waited until the peak of the season the following summer before she took a spade again to my father's grave. She smuggled his ghost back into the hotel without any of the headaches or complaints that she usually used to announce his approach.

I went to her room one morning with a cup of tea and found her crouching behind the door. Her hair was glued to her forehead. There were bubbles in the corner of her mouth.

"Where's your father?" she hissed as I offered her the cup.

I shook my head.

"He's hiding in the bathroom," she snapped.

I nodded.

"Why doesn't he help me with the breakfast?" she inquired bitterly.

I shook my head again.

"He's too drunk to fry eggs," she shouted.

I placed the saucer over the cup and laid it down beside the bed. When I turned to face her she gave me a sly glance that I did not trust. She looked so cunning that I thought her madness might be no more than a threat, a morbid method she had devised for winning a day in bed. I smiled. She replied with a horrible mocking grin. She was wearing a dressing-gown the colour of gravy. She hoisted the collar round her face.

"Don't worry," I said gently. I was looking at my mother but I was talking to myself.

I crept downstairs to the kitchen. It was very depressing. As I boiled the water I kept glancing across my shoulder, hoping to see her walk through the door, sensible and smiling. She would not leave me to manage the hotel alone. As I sliced the bread my hands started to tremble impatiently and I wanted to run back up the stairs, grab her by the shoulders and shake her from the trance before she sank too deep and was completely lost to me. But I had to wait. I had to wait until the breakfasts were finished and every last guest had been seen safely off the premises before I could go back to her room. And when I finally opened her door she had gone.

The sight of the empty room made the hair bristle on the back of my neck. There was no hope in pretending she was suffering from anxiety or fatigue. She was not asking for a day in bed with lunch on a tray. Her brains were scrambled. I was looking for a crazy woman with a meat axe in her fist. I tiptoed through the hotel, peering under beds and tables, whispering her name. But my mother had vanished. She had escaped. She was probably already running, screaming, along the beach with her dressing-gown wrapped around her head. I locked myself in the attic and tried to calm myself. I didn't know how to recapture her or where to turn for help. It was terrible.

Figg found my mother again. They met in the street, Figg trotting towards the hotel with her nylon coat on her arm and mother marching away from it with a blanket thrown round her shoulders. I don't know how Figg managed it but she brought the old lady home and helped me put her to bed. Then she slipped into her nylon coat and began to clean the kitchen as if nothing had happened.

It was several days before Figg mentioned the incident again. In the past she had always remained passive when confronted with my mother's peculiar antics and preferred to forget them. But this time I could see that even she had been impressed by the spectacle of my mother foaming at the mouth and roaming the streets in her dressing-gown. We were hard at work polishing the huge mirror that hung in the breakfast room when she finally spoke about it.

"Don't you think you should send for the doctor, Mr Burton?" she suggested casually as she smeared her reflection with Windolene.

"He came yesterday," I sighed.

"What did he say?"

"He told her to lie down and stay calm," I panted as I bullied the Windolene into the glass with my duster.

"But she hasn't been out of bed since we put her there," said Figg, frowning at herself through the smear.

It was true. My mother had taken the doctor's advice seriously and had barely moved a muscle since his visit. She lay on her back and stared at the ceiling in silence. She ate whatever I left on a tray and refused to utter a word.

"The cure could take months," I shrugged and shook my duster.

"But you can't manage the hotel alone, Mr Burton," Figg protested.

I rubbed at the mirror with my duster until I had cleaned a round spyhole about the size of my fist in the pink sludge. I pretended to polish it while I squinted at Figg through the flapping of the duster.

She was standing beside me and staring at the duster in her hands. Her face was very flushed and the eyebrows arched so high they were hidden by her hair. The fat little mouth had popped in surprise. I massaged away at the Windolene until I had uncovered Figg's shoulders and breasts. I rubbed at them gently until I found the courage to speak.

"I was hoping," I said at last, "I was hoping you could move in here for the summer . . ."

There was a long and terrible silence. We disguised our fright with a ferocious attack upon the mirror, scrubbing at the silver as if it might dissolve and let us pass through to the other side.

"I don't know . . . it won't be easy," panted Figg.

"There's a very cosy bedroom in the attic," I said. My heart was pounding and I had trouble trying to control my voice.

Figg said nothing.

"And, of course, there would be an increase in your wages," I added casually, as I caught her engagement ring winking at me.

"Well, I don't know – I should have to ask my mother," she said doubtfully and I knew she was counting the cost of her wedding dress.

"No, forget it," I said briskly. "I know it's impossible. I shouldn't try to burden you with my problems. I'm sorry." I stepped back from the mirror and turned towards the door.

Figg dropped her duster in alarm. "Oh, no . . . I would be glad to help you, Mr Burton," she stammered and clutched at my arm.

"Thank you," I whispered and smiled mournfully.

Figg was mine for the rest of the summer! It had been easier to entice her into the attic than I had expected and the arrangement worked perfectly. She worked beside me from dawn until dusk and then spent her evenings with Percy. He must have been excited by her flight from the nest but she never allowed him to take advantage of it. She always came home at night and never invited him to step inside the front door. It must have driven him wild to know that when they parted she trotted back to me for her hot milk and biscuits.

I was determined to give Figg my attic room because I wanted her to sleep in my bed. Of course, it meant that I would be forced to sleep on a broken sofa in some dusty store room at the back of the house. But it was worth the discomfort. Each night I lay down among the cobwebs and the broken springs and fired my dreams with the thought of the enormous Figg rolling naked in my sheets. I hoped that her weight would leave an impression in my mattress so that, when I returned to the bed again, I would be able to sleep in the hollow. I hoped that her perfume would stain the pillows so that when I pressed my face against them again I should be able to capture something of her body. I hoped that she would bewitch my room.

One evening, after Figg had gone to keep her appointment with Percy Pig, I stole into the attic to see if the magic had worked. She had arrived the previous week with nothing more than a large suitcase but her effect upon my room was astonishing. The carpet was covered in spilled shoes. On a chair beside the bed a bunch of abandoned underwear. Huge and heavy blossoms of cotton and lace. Upon the pillows of the bed a chocolate satin nightgown. A picture of a kingfisher, cut from a magazine and pasted on cardboard, had been pinned to the wall beside the window. Beneath the window my table was smothered in make-up and combs and ribbons. And everywhere the smell of her perfume teased me with its peppery sweetness.

The bed was unmade and, to my delight, the sheets contained a ditch the size and shape of the nocturnal Figg. I studied the ditch carefully, tracing the crumpled sheets with my fingers, as if I might uncover the most subtle contours of her body in the linen. And I knew that I was not merely running my hand through an empty bed but stroking the most lovely naked phantom and violating the object of Percy's ugliest dreams. It was enough to force an entry into Figg's private room but it was exquisite to know that, in the same moment, I was also robbing Percy's dreams of their treasure. I was walking where Percy was forbidden to tread. I was rummaging through the secrets Percy was forbidden to discover.

Those ten minutes spent poking around the attic room gave me a more intimate knowledge of the young Wendy Figg than Percy could acquire in ten years of struggling to force his hand up her skirt on some deserted patch of wet sand. While Figg lived in the hotel she belonged to me.

My mother, for her part, accepted Figg in the family without protest. She stayed in her room, took her meals from a tray and generally allowed me to take charge of the hotel. I think she was grateful for the opportunity to rest and read her books.

She certainly did nothing to upset the routine and, apart from the brief tantrums she liked to perform for the benefit of the doctor when he made a visit, she remained docile and mute.

She did not recover from her madness until November when the hotel was empty and Figg had gone home to her mother. Then her head seemed to clear as the first winter frost began to bite. It was a remarkable recovery. But, as I expected, when the storms died down in the Atlantic they grew again in my mother's head and at Easter she was confined once more to her bed. Figg came back to live in the attic and Percy Pig stalked the street outside, muttering darkly to himself.

This arrangement continued for three or four years and might have lasted forever but for the nasty nature of Percy Pig. I had prevented him from mauling the apple of his eye for too long and one night he told Figg their engagement was finished. There was a brief but violent battle in which she threw the cauliflower ring at him and he stamped on it, she slapped his ears and he kicked her ankles, she pulled him to the ground and he screamed beneath her weight. Poor Figg staggered home with her dress torn and blood beneath her fingernails.

I tried to comfort her with hot milk and brandy while she blubbered out her story.

"Don't cry, dear Figg. He isn't worth so many tears," I said gently as I helped her into a chair.

"Oh, Mr Burton, I was so frightened. He shouted at me and used bad language."

"What did he say to you?" I asked, wondering if I should risk wrapping her sympathetically into my arms and deciding that it was too early in the game.

"I don't know," she wailed. "But it was something filthy. And then . . . he hit me."

"Why, that's terrible!" I exploded. "A man should never hit a woman." Unless she throws the first punch, I thought. "It's unforgivable. He should be locked away. He's worse than a wild animal."

"An animal – that's exactly how he behaved," whimpered

Figg, her eyes glittering. "He was like an animal. My mother would kill me if she knew what happened . . . she told me he was only interested in the beast between his legs. He always pestered me. I should have known he was violent."

"You're safe now – blow your nose and drink your milk."

"Oh, Mr Burton, you're so kind to me. You're such a gentle person."

"You mustn't think that all men are monsters," I said. Her dress had burst along one seam and her thigh bulged softly through the torn stitches.

"I can't understand it. I never denied him anything. He was so impatient. If only he had waited just a little bit longer. I *wanted* to marry him. And now . . . and now . . ." She wrapped herself in her arms and rocked back and forth in the chair. The stitches in her dress began to creak and unravel towards her knee.

"Are you hurt? Perhaps I should take a look at you?" I said hopefully.

"No," blubbered Figg. "It's nothing. I just want to go to bed."

I gave her a handful of aspirins and helped her to the attic. But she did not sleep and long after midnight I heard her weeping in the rafters. I sat in my pyjamas and cursed Percy for the heartache he had caused. It was the height of the season and I could not run the hotel alone.

Finally I crept up to her room and pressed my face against the door, listening to the pathetic wails and snorts beyond. I wanted to soothe her pains and help her forget it. I could not leave her to her misery. So I opened the door and stepped inside. The room was in darkness but I knew the tread of every floorboard and easily tiptoed to the bed. The victim of Percy's abuse was buried beneath a blanket with a pillow pulled over her head. There was enough moonlight from the window to distinguish her bulk from the shape of the surrounding furniture. I stood there in my bare feet and peered at the heaving blanket. She was snorting so loudly she had not heard me enter the room. Perhaps I should have introduced myself with a short cough or a tap on the door. Instead I prised open an edge of the blanket and crawled inside. I found Figg's shoulder and gave it a gentle squeeze.

Figg's shoulder quivered as if she had been electrocuted, her head jumped out from under the pillow and she screamed. I cupped my hand across her mouth, trying to calm her and stop the scream before it reached the guests. But in my haste I speared a nostril with my thumb and she started to struggle.

It was the appropriate moment to identify myself, find Figg's ear and whisper something suitably apologetic into it. But in the excitement she had twisted her head back into the pillow and her ears were stuffed with feathers. She stopped screaming. But I could not surrender my grip for fear she might cripple me. She stopped struggling. But beneath the satin nightdress she felt so loose and hot that I could not pull my hands away. Her skin clung to my fingers like dough.

We lay together moaning gently when she suddenly began to paddle with her feet, banging her heels into my ribs. Her foot caught in the cord of my pyjamas and tore them apart. I tried to catch her by the toes but she was too strong for me and kicked me onto the floor. Frantic that she might escape from the attic and raise the alarm, I snatched at her ankle and dragged her with me as I fell from the bed.

"I love you," I wheezed as we rolled together. It sounded a trifle foolish but I was a desperate man.

Figg spluttered, sat on my chest and held my head between her knees. The nightdress was dragged up round her waist. Her belly rumbled in fury. I was afraid that she might open her thighs and swallow me for, as I stared, I fancied I saw the whiskery chin of some old man she had already swallowed wedged between them. Gradually she squeezed her knees together until I choked. And then, as if the life were flickering out of me, I saw Dorothy drift past my eyes. Little Dorothy wriggling and shrieking in the corner of my aunt's wardrobe as I had tried to wash her legs with my tongue. It was an inspiration! My tongue flopped out. But when I managed to smack it wetly against Figg's knees she picked me up by the ears and cracked my head against the floor. My teeth were sharp. My mouth was full of blood.

"I love you," I moaned as she dragged me up to kiss the old man's chin and threw me down to hit the floor.

Figg bellowed and continued to bang my head.

"I love you," I gurgled and tried to escape in a faint.

Through the banging and the blood I heard the clatter of a bell and my mother shouting for help.

At the sound of the bell Figg stopped battering my brains and let my head drop from her hands. We had woken my mother from the sparkling madness of her dreams and now she was trying to wake up the town. Figg stood up and tottered silently to the bed where she fell in an attitude of rigid surrender. Her eyes were screwed shut, her legs were open and the old man's chin tilted at the ceiling. I think she was waiting for the police.

I scrambled from the floor, kicked the shredded pyjamas from my ankles, caught them in my hand and ran from the attic. When I reached my room I snapped on the lights, locked the door and inspected my wounds in the mirror. My tongue had stopped bleeding and my ears were not torn. It wasn't too bad. I dressed carefully, combed my hair and went to calm my mother.

As I hurried along the corridor I heard the muffled roar of the guests as they crowded outside in the street, squinting up at the hotel, waiting for flames to spit from the windows. The building had been evacuated, doors were open and lights blazed. When I reached my mother I found her standing on her dressing-table, swinging the fire bell in her fist. It took some time to tempt her back into bed and it was dawn before I managed to do the same for our guests. Some of them refused to stay, packed immediately and stormed off in search of other hotels. The rest cautiously returned to their rooms and locked their doors. No one asked for breakfast.

Figg vanished. Later that day, when I finally found the courage to return to the attic it was empty. Nothing of Figg remained. There were fresh sheets on the bed and the kingfisher had been torn from the wall. The window was open.

The spell she had cast on my attic had been broken.

My mother, true to her nature, waited until absolute calm had been restored before she broke out again. She had failed to set the hotel alight by sounding the alarm so next she built a bonfire in the bathroom and set fire to it. The smoke whispered its way through the keyhole, down the long stairs and into the kitchen before it found me. When I broke down the door I found a mattress burning in the bath and my mother trying to feed it with scraps of paper. She screamed when she saw me. Her fingers were black with soot and her cardigan stank of paraffin. I dragged her out of the bathroom and tied her safely into a chair. Then I smothered the blaze and called the doctor.

Rudolph Ripley had been our doctor for a long time and was keenly interested in my mother's condition so that, once I had telephoned, he was on the doorstep within minutes. He was a tall, unhealthy specimen who traded in tonics and tranquillisers. I don't believe he was a very good doctor but he was always popular because he sat and listened to your complaints and never failed to give you a prescription. You could tell him you had maggots in your ears and he'd give you something for them. He was that kind of doctor.

When he looked at my mother he promptly stuck a needle in her arm and picked the ashes from her hair. I knew what he was going to tell me but I waited in silence, watching him grope for the words. People love to announce bad news and I could see that he was enjoying himself. He sighed and shook his head. He stood up and sat down. He coughed a few times, as if he were trying to tune his voice.

"It would be best for everyone if your mother were admitted to hospital," he said finally. "Believe me, she needs proper treatment. I appreciate that you've tried to do your best for her these last few years – and it can't have been easy – but it wasn't fair to expect a young man of your age to play nurse."

I did not argue with him. We were sitting on the edge of the bed, staring at the toasted bundle of dressing-gown and old cardigans that we liked to call my mother. She was still tied by the wrists to the chair. Her head was resting on one shoulder and her mouth was open. She was snoring peacefully. The noise of it reminded me of Figg blubbering as I had tried to comfort her with my warmth. The knowledge that I might never again follow the rustle of her nylon coat from room to room or peep between the cracks of her straining buttons made me burst into tears.

Rudolph Ripley seemed pleased with my performance. He fished in the pockets of his coat and produced a tobacco tin full of fat, white pills. He offered me one and I placed it forlornly on the tip of my tongue. It was a peppermint.

"It's a wonderful hospital, believe me. The doctors are good, the gardens are beautiful and the food is excellent. In fact, you shouldn't think of it as a hospital – think of it as a very quiet hotel." He started to laugh at his little joke and then, remembering his surroundings, stopped and pretended to choke.

"How long do you think she'll be away?" I asked him, wiping my nose in my hand.

He shook his head. "Don't expect any improvements overnight, William," he whispered. I smiled bravely and cracked the peppermint with my teeth.

It was a long and bitter winter. I lived alone in the hotel, sleeping in a different room each night, hoping to keep the building alive. I imagined that without a little human heat percolating through its damp walls the hotel would die of neglect. I left the lights burning. I carried a radio wherever I went and played music so loudly it created draughts and shocked the dust from the furniture. I slammed doors and stamped on carpets. But despite my furious efforts I could feel the hotel sinking around me. When I sat in the attic I thought I could hear the basement moaning and when I went to comfort the basement I could only hear rain on the attic window. Gradually the hotel was sinking into a cold sleep and I knew I was sinking with it.

I was not lonely. I began making plans for the future and dreaming of adventures in the outside world. I could not guess that I was destined to become a monster, a loathsome creature of the night. I thought I might be a ventriloquist. In the evenings I sat and gave my voice wings so that it flew from room to room, calling my name and answering to the echo. My talents were enough to prompt me to look for a doll to sit on my knee and engage in conversation.

There is magic in a ventriloquist's doll. They are not crude puppets to be jiggled on your fingers and thrown into boxes. A doll is given the breath of life and must be treated with some respect. There are not many such dolls made orphan in a seaside town during winter, but I owned a complete harem of stunted scarecrows.

I remembered all of them. There was Brenda Thistle, a midget made from a tea towel and a pair of cotton gloves; Monica Potts, a friendly trollop with a slippery body sewn from a pink silk petticoat; Pansy Stone, a nasty piece of work with hideous hearth rug hair; and my childhood sweetheart Nectarine Summers with her sly button eyes and the biggest buttocks in toyland.

These faithful rag dolls were still buried in a trunk in the attic. Brenda fell apart in my hands and something had eaten Pansy's hair but Nectarine Summers was safely plucked from the grave. She was larger than her companions, a limp yet heavy bundle with a crumpled face and huge thighs stuffed with feathers. Her nose had been cut from a wooden peg and her mouth was a line of crooked red stitches. She was certainly no great beauty but when she sat on my knee we talked for hours.

When conversation failed we found other ways to keep ourselves amused. She was constantly amazed by my conjuring tricks. She watched, breathless, while I pulled eggs from my ears, ribbons from my nose, blew sparks and spat razor blades. Only for a moment did I consider that should anyone visit me without warning and see me sharing jokes with my doll they would think me as mad as my mother. The very next day I had visitors.

The doorbell rang in the afternoon. There were storms in the Atlantic, the sky was the colour of mustard and the street was black. I ran to hide Nectarine Summers under the stairs. When I drew back the bolts and opened the door two thin shadows confronted me.

"Hello, Mackerel. It's Dorothy," said one of the shadows. I stepped back in surprise, the two shadows trotted into the hall and stood beneath the electric light, waiting for my inspection.

The one called Dorothy was a lean woman in her late twenties. She wore a camelhair coat and grey leather shoes. There was still a trace of greyhound in her face but she had learnt to conceal it with powder and paint. She introduced the second shadow as her husband and he thrust out his hand. I shook it briefly and he placed it carefully in his pocket. He was gaunt and losing his hair. He wore a crinkled suit beneath a brand new Burberry.

"You won't remember me," Dorothy crooned. "I helped your aunt look after you when your father died. It was a long time ago. You were only a child."

I had forgotten nothing. "How is my aunt?" I asked with a smile.

"She's dead," said the husband.

I stopped smiling.

"I'm sorry," said Dorothy. They both looked as if they expected me to panic and piddle on my shoes.

"Would you like a cup of tea?" I inquired after a long pause.

They nodded their heads and followed me into the kitchen.

"Where's your mother?" asked Dorothy as she unbuttoned her coat.

"She went mad," I said cheerfully and filled the kettle.

"I'm sorry," said the husband. He looked tragic, as if he held himself personally responsible for all the unhappiness in the world. He sat down exhausted at the table while Dorothy helped me make the tea.

It was the saddest feeling to see her again. Did she remember our antics in the great wardrobe? It was impossible that she could have forgotten – she had *invented* the game. Yet she gave me no sign. She gazed at me with the placid eyes of a smug young wife. She was not distant but she was far from flirtatious. Everything about her was cool and measured. She expressed sympathy for me and concern for my mother, a polite interest in the fate of the hotel and a general interest in the weather. There was nothing in her attitude to suggest that we had once washed each other with our tongues and promised to die in each other's arms.

The husband, however, was soon talking to me as if we were the most intimate friends. His name was Archie and he owned a string of butchers' shops. He pulled off his Burberry, dropped it on the floor and spoke at great length about the mysteries of meat. It was an education. I found a bottle of wine and encouraged him to talk about his art. After he had drunk most of the bottle he became so excited that he made me go tramping with him through the town in search of steak which we carried home to fry.

Archie laid the steak out on the kitchen table to watch it bleed. I stood behind him with a frying pan in my hands while Dorothy sat and merely smiled.

"Meat is life," Archie said gravely. "Life is meat."

He stretched out one hand and gave the meat a prod with a blunt finger. The frying pan was swinging softly in my hands.

"We are born and we are eaten," Archie continued. "This is known as a natural cycle. There is no waste involved in a natural cycle." He was very drunk. I think he was reciting the butcher's prayer.

He picked up the meat, held it away from the table and we stared at the puddle of blood. The blood began to roll towards the floor. The frying pan began to rise towards the meat.

"Blood thickens gravy," said Archie. "Gravy thickens meat. There's an end to it." He folded the meat carefully into the metal pan and moved away to fry it.

We drank more wine and ate the meat with our fingers, according to his instructions. Even Dorothy seemed to relax a little and laughed and smeared her chin with blood. Afterwards they asked me more about my mother and I told them the whole story. Dorothy clucked and shook her head. Archie was so impressed he insisted that we visit the hospital the following day. So I asked them to be my guests for the night.

I found fresh sheets and blankets and led them to their room. Archie sat on the end of the bed, waved me goodnight and looked for his feet. Dorothy smiled and closed the door.

As soon as I thought they were asleep I crept downstairs and retrieved Nectarine Summers from her hiding place. We sat together in the kitchen and I told her of my visitors. She thought them a strange couple, he with his big, slow hands and bovine face and she with her manners and sharp, little teeth. But I told her of the wardrobe days and Dorothy's erotic cruelty. It was natural, I explained, that she should marry a man who also loved corpses, a man who softened his hands in pigs' entrails and could be moved to tears by the succulent beauty of a raw kidney. Well, Nectarine Summers took some convincing but, in the end, she agreed with me. We sat in the dark and speculated gleefully on the unspeakable rituals of their marriage bed.

Archie drove us to the hospital late the following morning. It was a large country house in the middle of nowhere, surrounded by trees and rough lawn. It was a handsome building with an atmosphere of picturesque decay. It might have been a school or a small museum.

No one greeted us at the door so we crept inside and began to search the corridors for a doctor or nurse. But no one came to our rescue and we finally reached a recreation room full of televisions and yellow newspapers. There were three or four truculent girls sitting at a table rolling cigarettes. They sneered at us when we passed but said nothing. One of them crossed herself and tapped the table.

I found my mother sitting alone in a corner of the room. She was wearing several cardigans and a pair of old trousers. She did not recognise me. I knelt down beside her and held her hand. She looked at me with mild suspicion but did not pull her hand away.

"Is that your mother?" whispered Archie amazed.
"Yes," I said, "I recognise her cardigans."
"I don't think she's going to talk to you," whispered Dorothy doubtfully.
"I expect she's waiting for my father," I said.
Then Dorothy presented my mother with a big bunch of flowers. Red and white carnations in a damp paper cone. My mother accepted them with a strange smile. She held them in both hands and pushed her nose into them. She began to eat them. She bit off their heads and ate them. The red ones seemed to be her favourite.
I sat and watched my mother eat while Dorothy and Archie went in search of a doctor. When they eventually found one he was reluctant to voice an opinion about the state of my mother's brains. He had an arrogant tilt to his chin and kept cocking his head as we talked to him. Beneath his white coat he sported an expensive suit and a brand new pair of suede shoes. You can't trust a man who wears suede shoes. When I asked him when I could take the old lady home he looked surprised.
"She's one of our favourites," he said, "We'd be sorry to see her leave."
"Yes, but when can we take her home?" insisted Archie.
"She wouldn't be happy outside," the doctor declared with a brief smile.
"But she can't be happy here," snapped Dorothy.
The doctor turned upon Dorothy, cocked his head this way and that to inspect her from the top of her head to the tip of her toes. He had his hands in his pockets. He began to jangle some coins with his fingers.
"I find that a very offensive remark, young lady. Our patients are kept under the strictest medical supervision. We pride ourselves on our standards of discipline and hygiene. We're a family. Doctors and patients together," he said coldly.
"She doesn't need another family," said Archie stubbornly. "We want to take her home."
The doctor sighed, pulled a hand from his pocket and glan-

ced at his wristwatch.

"Perhaps you'd better come into my office," he said, "Follow me."

He led us down a maze of gloomy corridors and unlocked a heavy panelled door. The office was large and comfortable, Indian carpets on the floor, Victorian watercolours on the walls, several narrow wooden chairs, and one huge leather chair behind a polished oak desk. The doctor arranged himself behind the desk and invited us to sit before him. He picked up a fountain pen and began to roll it between his fingers. It was some moments before he spoke.

"This hospital cares for depressed and confused people," he said carefully. "It's not a prison for the violent and the raving. We think of it as a shelter, a special place where people can come and rest and sort themselves out."

"You can't lock people up forever just because they're depressed," said Dorothy, "I get depressed. He gets depressed," she said, pointing a finger at me. "It's a very depressing world."

The doctor continued rolling the pen in his hand. He was not impressed by Dorothy's outburst.

"There are no locks or bars in this hospital. As I've tried to explain, it's not a prison."

"Then we'd like to take the old lady home," said Archie.

The doctor threw the butcher a withering glance and the butcher cracked his knuckles loudly. He wasn't going to be bullied by a man who wore suede shoes.

"You don't seem to understand me," said the doctor. "The patient – my patient – is receiving a complicated drug therapy treatment. It would be dangerous to remove her from here for at least twelve months. Perhaps longer . . ."

"Poking drugs down her throat won't make the world any less depressing," muttered Archie. Dorothy gave him a long, hard stare.

"You mentioned that you suffered from depressive anxiety," the doctor said softly.

"Who?" I said, looking up in alarm. "No, I don't think I said that . . ."

"Was your father an anxious man?"

"I don't remember," I said with a frown.

"His father is dead," explained Dorothy.

"Have you had treatment for any depressive illness in the past?" inquired the doctor, tapping his pen against the desk.

"No."

"Were you depressed or anxious when you learned that your mother would need hospital treatment?"

"Yes, of course, it was very sad," I said.

"And that's why you're here today?" he asked gently.

"Yes."

The doctor nodded his head and began to roll the pen once more between his fingers. He smiled. "Perhaps we should make an appointment for you to visit us again . . ."

"Why?" I said.

"I'd like to talk to you. I think I could help you," said the doctor cryptically.

"Come on, Mackerel. Let's go home," snorted Dorothy in great disgust.

We stood up and marched from the office. The doctor did nothing to block our retreat. We marched away through the maze of corridors, losing our way, retracing our steps, swearing and kicking at doors. We drove home in silence. It was very depressing.

After Dorothy's brief visit to the hotel I felt lonely and suffocated in the dusty shadows of my room. I felt that, somehow, I had been left behind. Dorothy had sprouted into the world and even penetrated the mysteries of marriage while I remained at home, a pale and curious dwarf of a man. The empty hotel began to depress me and I took to walking the cliffs each evening in an effort to think about myself and escape the brooding ghost of my mother. I left Nectarine Summers in our favourite kitchen chair and went walking for hours with nothing but the sound of the sea washing around inside my head.

It was time to make something of my life. I wanted to invent some new and daring feat of magic that would baffle audiences across the world. I saw myself alone on a spotlit stage holding thousands enchanted with the William Burton Blazing Wardrobe or the Burton Pyramid of Nails.

Beyond the promenade and a narrow stretch of beach the cliffs reared into a huge rollercoaster of rock. There were narrow footpaths cut along the very edge of these cliffs, which were so high that when I walked them it was like walking in the sky with nothing but the moon to guide my feet. I walked with the wind scratching my face and gulped at the clean, sharp air. I walked and waited for an inspiration that would help me make sense of my life.

One evening, as I was struggling towards the highest ledge, I saw a figure moving towards me. At first it was no more than a small, black exclamation mark bobbing against the slate of the sky. But as it drew closer it developed legs and an overcoat. I stopped walking and watched it approach. There was something familiar about the tilt of the head and the thrust of the shoulders but it was not until the figure was almost upon me that I recognised him.

It was Percy Pig. There was no mistake. It was Percy fighting his way along the track with his hands in his pockets and his face pushed into his coat. Stray rings of hair flopped damply around his collar. I stepped aside to let him pass and, as he drew level with me, he glanced up and sneered. Did he recognise me or was it the force of the wind in his face that made him pull back his lips to reveal that mouthful of broken teeth? Had he forgiven Figg and been told of my assault on her prostrate person? Or did he mourn her loss even now, and exercise his grief at night upon these cliffs? It was a mystery. I turned towards him but he moved away.

And then it happened. I wanted to say something to him. I wanted to reach out and touch him. But when I stretched out my hand and caught his collar he seemed to twist upon his heel. He threw out his arms. His feet did a mad little dance. He danced sideways off the edge of the cliff and disappeared. I edged my way to the brink of the cliff and stared into the boiling sea beneath me. Percy was gone. I couldn't believe it had happened. It had been so quick. I stood blinking into the water as if he might surface and offer me a cheerful wave of his hand. But Percy Pig had vanished.

I ran home to Nectarine Summers and told her what had happened. But, for the first time in her life, she had nothing to say for herself. Her mouth was stitched shut and there were no words of comfort. She stared at me like a bundle of old rags. It was as if my magic was suddenly too potent for the dainty manipulation of dolls. I had discovered, in those few brief moments on the cliff, the magic of life and death, the ultimate disappearing trick, the ability to snuff out lives like candles. And now, the hands that had first tickled life into Nectarine Summers seemed to draw that life from her again. She was dead. She was nothing but an armful of feathers and dust. I dumped her on the kitchen table and searched the cupboards for brandy. My fingers were trembling and cold. When I tried to pour the brandy into a cup I splashed my wrists. It was hopeless. I plugged the bottle into my mouth, threw back my head and let the brandy pour down my throat. I was waiting for the police to arrive and arrest me. Once the brandy had warmed me I went upstairs, took a bath and changed into my best suit.

It was important to create the right impression when they came knocking at the door. I did not want them to think I was a criminal. So I shaved carefully and sucked a peppermint to sweeten my breath. Then I staggered into the breakfast room where I hid behind the curtains and watched the street. It was raining and the town was deserted. The silence was so deep that I wondered again if I had really met Percy Pig on that lonely clifftop track or merely imagined him. Perhaps I was to be cursed with the ghost of Percy as my mother was haunted by the ghost of my father. Had he been no more than a vivid memory given shape for a moment by the twisted rocks and the flight of the wind? He had not been flesh and bone. I had not thrown him into the sea. I stood beside the window for hours, denying any knowledge of our fatal encounter until eventually I fell asleep.

When I woke up I found myself on the floor beneath the curtains. I continued to hide there all morning and in the afternoon crept out to buy a newspaper to read of Percy's death. I expected to see his photograph on the front page but he was nowhere to be found. I picked my way through the newspaper, inch by inch, but there was no mention of the corpse. Perhaps poor Percy had been swept out to sea and was floating peacefully for America. I felt a little more optimistic about the interview with the police. It might take weeks for Percy to make the return voyage and, by then, he would never be recognised. But if the police finally seized me I would confess everything. I was prepared for their interrogation.

Yes, I was walking along the cliffs on that particular night. No, the dead man was a stranger to me. Yes, I saw him leap from the ledge and disappear into the sea. No, I did not run for assistance because I did not believe the evidence of my own eyes. Yes, I had been drinking and depressed because of my mother's failing state of health. I want to confess that at the time I was considering my own suicide.

I rehearsed these answers with an expression of startled innocence. I was shocked by their questions and concerned for the relatives of the deceased. I had no good reason to throw Percy Pig into the sea. And without a motive there could be no crime. I knew I would be just another name on a long sheet of names that the police would investigate. And I could give them no reason for suspicion or alarm.

It was a week before Percy made his final appearance. He was washed onto the beach and the newspaper described it as a misadventure. No one thought it remarkable that a man should fall from the cliffs and drown. When I read the news I felt almost disappointed. They say that your first murder is the most important moment in your life. The first murder is the one that usually kills you with guilt or grief. Most men follow murder with suicide. Yet I cannot say that I was tormented in the knowledge that I had killed Percy. On reflection, it could hardly be described as a murder.

But it was a beginning. I had discovered the secret of a new and terrible conjuring trick. And, in the manner of all magicians, I wanted to master it. When I next walked through the town I found myself selecting suitable victims, following them down the street and choosing my moment to reveal an imaginary revolver or knife. Blades sprang from the tips of my shoes. Acid spat from my buttonhole. My thumbs were loaded pistols. I slaughtered men and women at random and watched them roll in the gutter, their mouths were full of blood and their faces were white with amazement. It was a macabre game for a bright young man. But in these rehearsals it was not William Mackerel Burton, but the Sandman himself walking down the street, throwing the dust of sleep in the face of the crowd. Do you understand? It wasn't murder. It was magic.

The Sandman sat in the empty hotel and prepared himself for his life's work. The body of Nectarine Summers had fallen under the kitchen table and my first task was to give her a decent burial. I wrapped the corpse in a black chiffon scarf, a gift to my mother from Uncle Eno, and carried her down to the basement boiler. The fire was very low but the ashes were hot. I kissed her one last time and pushed her carefully into the ashes. The scarf shrank into a luminous cinder and floated away. I waited until the smoke was curling from her seams and I knew that the biggest buttocks in toyland were ready to explode. I quickly closed the boiler door. Nectarine Summers was gone.

You may blame the death of my father or my mother's madness for the choice of career. You may blame Dorothy's necrophilia or Blakey's skill as a conjurer. It is not important. I sold the hotel shortly after Christmas. I was not a rich man as a result but I was determined to indulge my dangerous pursuit without the hindrance of honest employment in an office or a factory. I instructed the bank to provide the hospital with whatever funds they required for my mother's comfort and then I set out for London and the killing ground.

The city overwhelmed me. Here were millions of strangers endlessly jostling through the dirty, deafening streets. Millions of grey strangers with vacant eyes. Every day a few of them would fall, or be pushed, out of trains, under buses, off rooftops, through windows and into the grave. It made no difference. There were so many of them. You could scoop up ten thousand and still make no space on the streets. No matter how you kicked or stamped on this huge ant heap you could never diminish the wriggling black mass of it.

For the first few weeks I could not walk the streets without feeling myself tremble in excitement at the expression on the face of the crowd. It was an expression of misery, as if life were something to be hated, a punishment or a disease. I thought, if these strangers could have life painlessly removed from their veins they would probably stand in line outside the hospitals. I thought, if it were made possible tonight, by some simple magic, for them to die in their sleep, they would go home laughing and scramble into pyjamas. And the magic had arrived among them.

I rented an apartment a few minutes' walk from Victoria Station. Killers, I knew from my boyhood visits to the cinema, dwelt in basements ugly as caves, full of broken bottles and bundles of damp newspaper. They crouched at smeared windows and stared up at the feet of the people who passed on the street above. If they could not find a basement they might accept an attic with a crumbling fire escape that led nowhere and the blistering glare of neon light through the curtains at night. The rooms I chose for myself were small and exquisitely pretty. The chairs were sweet and plump. The carpets sighed ecstatically when you trod on them. Here I would sit and contemplate murder in comfort.

As soon as I was settled into my rooms I set out to explore the little kingdom of Victoria. I began each morning outside the station with its fine white stone and red brick facade, its countless windows and tall chimneys. I would enter through the grand arch where bare-breasted mermaids smirk down from their perch at the tired and worried office workers crowded blindly beneath them. I would stroll then beneath the enormous glass ceiling and watch the trains leave for Europe and the South. There is a tunnel cut through the station wall beside Platform Three. The tunnel leads into Wilton Road and when I was finished with the station I would leave through this tunnel and turn sharp right, walking towards Hudson's Depository that stands against the street like a tall wedge of grey cheese. I have always loved the strange flavour of Wilton Road; the Mambo Café and the barber's shop, Woolworth and the Biograph, the novelty joke shop and the Sultan Massage Parlour. I would turn right into Gillingham Street and then follow the London Transport Garage out towards Warwick Square. Here, behind the station and stretching down to the Thames, are wide streets of mouldering houses and cheap hotels, odd terraces of brick cottages, grubby groceries, empty churches and travel agencies with their windows full of dusty cardboard. It is old and shabby and full of discreet decay. I walked down every street and alley until I knew Victoria like my own hand.

At first, everyone in this great city was a stranger. But, gradually, some of the faces on the streets repeated themselves until I learned to distinguish between the local population and the grey, blank expressions of the office workers and travellers. My neighbours also made themselves known to me.

Johnson Johnson lived directly beneath me and was always snooping outside my door or prowling about on the stairs. He lived with his mother who was small and wrinkled and very fierce. On the rare occasions I saw them together in the street she reminded me of a mad and hairy child being walked by a nurse. She had a face that resembled a diseased cauliflower and favoured white ankle socks and children's sandals. Johnson Johnson was nearly as ugly as his mother and, in the manner of all ugly men, he was very vain about his appearance. He kept a metal comb in his jacket pocket and could not walk past his reflection without pausing to preen his hair. He first introduced himself by knocking on my door one night and asking me to turn down the sound of my television for the sake of his mother's health. And, after that, he made regular visits with his little complaints. My drains were blocked. My pipes were banging. My floorboards creaked. My doors were slamming. He was polite but he annoyed me. I imagined the pair of them sitting beneath my floor with their heads cocked, charting my passage from room to room and waiting their chance to lodge a complaint.

Directly above me, in the attic, lived an old man called Tom

Larch. He took an immediate dislike to me for reasons I cannot fathom for I was always polite to him whenever our paths crossed. I was anxious, naturally, to avoid making enemies of my neighbours but as soon as I encountered Tom Larch I knew I could not trust him and I was not surprised to learn later that he was an old friend of Johnson Johnson's mother.

Beneath Johnson Johnson lived an American teacher called Frank, a mild-mannered man with an unusual appetite for women. But it was some time before I made his acquaintance. Beneath Frank, in the basement, lived an old lady with a family of cats. She rarely emerged into the daylight world and Frank tapped on her door once a week to see if she was still alive, although I never saw her in person and she might have been one of Frank's inventions.

It was in this small and peaceful colony that I sat and dreamed of murder.

Who should I bless with the kiss of death? It was simple. I would choose the most disagreeable face in the crowd. It was to be the swift and silent encounter between the one who could turn life into death and the one who looked as if they might welcome the change. I was impatient to practise my peculiar craft but it was important to find the right customer. It was a considerable challenge because no one looked especially enthusiastic about the prospect of remaining alive; but the moment I walked into the Empire Stores, Edgware Road, I knew my search was ended.

She was a tall, venomous woman with thick, black hair. At a glance she might have been thought a handsome woman but she made every effort to conceal it. She was probably no more than thirty years old, yet she already wore the expression of someone who feels cheated by life. Her eyes were bleary with malice and her mouth was primed to spit and snarl. It was such a vicious expression that her corner of the store was empty. No one dared to trespass in her territory. The Empire Stores sold everything from saucepans to sandals, but they had trouble selling *anything* within reach of this woman.

I strolled around for a few minutes and bought a cheap plastic raincoat – the kind that folds itself into a purse and tucks into your pocket. It was a translucent, bile green raincoat with a hood for the head. I spent some time pretending to hesitate between the bile green and the liver blue, but all the time I was watching the woman at the counter.

Finally I turned and presented her with the raincoat, fumbling for my wallet and slapping my pockets in an absent manner. I noticed she had a badge pinned to her coat. It read: Doris Forest Happy to Serve You. I smiled. She snarled, took the money and punched the raincoat into a bag. She held up the bag between finger and thumb and waved it at me. The expression on her face suggested she had just been tied to a chair and forced to endure some disgusting depravity at the hands of a madman. It was defiant yet slightly nauseated and her eye glittered with bitterness. I smiled again but she managed to ignore it.

I was reluctant to leave the store. It was almost closing time and the other counter girls were staring anxiously at the clock. If I was careful, I decided, I could follow Doris home. So I walked across the street and stood at a bus stop. It was the perfect hiding place. I had a good view of the Empire Stores and was soon rewarded by the sight of Doris Forest Happy to Serve You marching across the street towards me. She did not even look in my direction but immediately bullied her way to the front of the queue and stood stamping her feet impatiently. She had attractive legs with long, narrow ankles. She wore a demure cotton dress and had wrapped a jacket around her shoulders against the cool of the evening.

A convoy of buses roared into the kerb and there was a brisk scramble to board them. Doris was so quick that I almost lost her but I somehow managed to squeeze aboard and wedge myself in a seat. I could see Doris sitting at the front of the bus. She was glaring aimlessly at the other passengers. I was convinced that when she turned to leave she would recognise me, but there was nothing I could do to conceal myself. Indeed, when she left the bus in Kilburn High Street she brushed so close against me that I smelt her perfume. Yet she did not offer me a glance. She jumped from the bus and was already away down the street before my own feet had touched the ground.

It was getting dark. She hurried down a narrow street of dirty houses, turned sharply and disappeared through some broken railings. I strolled towards the spot where she'd gone to earth and glimpsed a flight of concrete stairs leading down from the street to a basement door. I did not hesitate. I am an artist. I walked to the corner before I turned and walked back along the street. As I passed the house again I glanced through the railings and into the basement. Doris Forest stood at the window, pulling the curtains against intruders. I felt rather pleased with myself. I had chosen a partner for my little dance of death. Her name was Doris Forest and she lived at the bottom of a house of rented rooms.

A casual exploration of the neighbourhood revealed a street that ran directly behind Doris Forest Street. An old warehouse stood in this street and, behind the warehouse, an overgrown yard glimpsed through a collapsed brick wall. It was black in the yard but a patch of bramble seemed to glow with a muddy yellow light. When I reached the light I found myself staring again into Doris Forest's basement! She had not bothered to close the curtains on this side of the house, believing herself to be hidden beneath the wall in the yard.

The rest of the building was in darkness and the undergrowth sheltered me from the eyes of prying neighbours. So I sat down among the brambles and watched the basement for nearly an hour. She seemed to use the back room as a kitchen and bathroom. The walls were a nasty shade of apricot and the floor was bare. There was a sink and a draining-board beneath the window and beyond a table and chair. A lamp with a pleated paper shade sat on the table. A threadbare dressing-gown slumped in the chair. Doris Forest moved back and forth, took off her shoes and yawned, washed her face and smoked a cigarette, wrapped herself in her dressing-gown and brewed a pot of tea. Then the light went out and there was nothing left but the faint blue blur of a television from another room.

I watched Doris Forest in her gloomy basement kitchen at

regular intervals for a fortnight before I made it the scene of my crime. While I sat in the brambles I tried to imagine what might happen to Doris if I saved her from murder. What other death would take my place if I turned and tiptoed home, denying her my magic touch? She would not be granted eternal life. I would hardly be saving her from the grave. Tomorrow she might poke her finger in the toaster and explode in flames. Drown in the bath. Fall down the stairs. She might suffer pneumonia or suffocate on fish bones. She might even take her own life, cut her wrists, choke on aspirin, plug the keyhole and turn on the gas.

Death is bewildering in its variety. And while I tried to estimate the chances of Doris surviving into ripe old age, the act of murder grew confused in my mind with the act of love. Every night, under cover of darkness, lovers perform a ritual murder. When a man and a woman roll naked together, what is their struggle but a pantomime of violence? And their moans of pleasure, what are they but whispered words of abuse? And that brief moment of capitulation, what is that but a fleeting glimpse of death? Smothered in each other's arms they fight to suck the breath from each other and threaten themselves with ecstasy. But they are content merely to rehearse this supreme act of lust. And I would, most certainly, send Doris Forest to paradise. Exactly. We would share the most intimate moment of her life and, when she fainted into my arms, it would be the ultimate surrender.

The moment arrived when I could no longer resist knocking on her door and introducing myself. Doris Forest had an appointment to keep with death and everything had been planned to the smallest detail.

The morning of the murder I couldn't eat anything but oranges and biscuits. I drank a lot of milk and sat in the bath. The thought of the coming night aroused in me a trembling love-sickness, fermented from a blend of pleasure and fear. I became as superstitious as a child, reading signs into the most trivial events, counting biscuit crumbs in my saucer, casting my fortune in the shadow of clouds against the wall of my room. There was magic in everything I saw and touched. In the afternoon I tried to sleep but my dreams were disturbed by an incubus who danced obscenely at the foot of my bed and I woke up shouting for Wendy Figg. It was not until the light faded at the window that I was able to take control of myself and concentrate all my nervous excitement into making the final preparations.

A little after seven o'clock I packed a Harrods shopping bag with a pair of kitchen rubber gloves, the bile green plastic raincoat and two lightweight butcher's knives. At seven-thirty I caught the bus from Victoria Station into Kilburn. I was wearing an old suit and a brand new pair of very cheap shoes. I had washed my hair and shaved.

Anything might have stopped me making that journey. The doubtful look of a stranger passing in the crowd, a shower of rain, the sight of the police on the street, anything might have saved me from murder. I would have turned around, gone home and taken up a career in the hotel business. But nothing happened and I reached the basement.

Under the shadow of the basement steps I dressed myself in the raincoat and rubber gloves. It was late in the game but even now, I told myself, if something went wrong I could retreat safely. If a stranger answered the door, or Doris was entertaining a lover, I would act simple and ask directions. Where is Paddington Cemetery? Where is the nearest police station? Anything. Easy. No harm done. I picked up my shopping bag and folded it carefully under my arm. I clenched my teeth. I rang the bell.

Nothing happened for a few moments and then I heard Doris barking at me through the door. I didn't understand a word of it. I said nothing. She rattled some chains and the door flew open. There was a rush of stale air, hot gravy, carpets and cheap perfume.

"You're early," Doris barked without looking at me. She was trying to hide behind the door and only her arm was visible, waving at me impatiently. The arm was naked and waving me forward so I stepped inside and closed the door.

Doris was standing in a narrow corridor. Her hair was wet and combed flat against her skull. Her face looked pale and damp. She was wearing nothing but a crumpled cotton sweater and a pair of slippers. The slippers were made from cardboard and nylon fur. She had pressed her spine against the wall and was bent forward slightly, clutching the hem of the sweater in a fist between her legs. The legs were the colour of porridge.

"Who the hell are you?" she demanded.

"Doris?" I enquired softly.

I stepped forward and she began to slide sideways along the wall, standing on tiptoe, her fists pressed deeper into her groin.

"What do you want?" she hissed.

"I've come for you, Doris," I said gently and smiled.

She fled to the nearest door and walked backwards into the bedroom.

"Get out!" she yelled. "What do you want?"

"I want to put you out of your misery, Doris."

The raincoat made crackling noises when I moved and my fingers were already hot and wet inside the rubber gloves.

"What misery? Who are you?" she demanded.

"Sit down," I said. She sat down in a big armchair beneath the window. She placed one foot upon the other and pressed her knees shut. It was then she became my victim. There was no reason why she should obey me. She could have ignored the instruction and fought her way into the street. She could have screamed and shouted for help. She could have simply started to laugh. But she sat down. And her obedience gave me her surrender.

"Don't be afraid," I said cheerfully and sat down myself on the edge of her bed.

She looked at me carefully for the first time. She surveyed the bile green coat and the lurid orange gloves. Then, to my dismay, I saw her expression gradually change from morbid fear to smothered anger. She obviously thought I was mad. She was going to humour me, calm me down, turn me around and smack my head with a frying pan. You could see it begin to smoulder in her eyes. She was already plotting murder.

"I'm not afraid," she said, "But tell me why you're here."

I didn't reply. I was looking around the room. It was much

more comfortable than I had imagined and, despite all the clothes scattered across the floor and the general disorder of the bed, it was clean and friendly.

"I was in the shower," Doris said cautiously, "Can I go and get dressed? I'm cold." She nodded towards the wardrobe and forced a smile.

I shook my head. She probably kept her frying pan in the wardrobe.

"I won't hurt you," she whispered. It was such a curious remark that I couldn't find a reply. There was a weird silence while I rummaged in the shopping bag for a knife. I pulled the blade from its sheath and stared at it. I didn't know where to begin.

There was a flurry of cushions and Doris had leapt from the chair and was running blindly towards the door. I was quick. I stood up and ran forward, the knife in my hand, my shoulder already against the door. But Doris did not stop running. She ran, she ran to embrace the knife, threw her arms around my neck and hung there breathless and surprised.

When she pulled away from me the raincoat made little kissing sounds where it clung to her skin. She stepped back, twisted on her heel and walked to the chair. She sat down again and looked at me. The knife was buried in her ribs. She stared down at the knife and smiled. She shook her head and smiled.

"You've stabbed me," she wheezed.

I stared at her in the shocking silence. She did not look angry. She looked as if nothing unusual had happened. Her hands were folded gently over her belly. But her hair was tangled and she had lost a slipper. I stared at the naked foot. There were traces of cracked nail varnish on her toes. I thought it was blood.

I knelt down beside her and stared at the knife for a long time. It had not been an ugly death. She looked as if she had fainted. Her mouth was hanging open and her eyes were closed. Her hair had dried into string. Death had not transformed her into a beauty but she certainly looked less dangerous than she had looked that afternoon in the Empire Stores. The face was peaceful and loose.

Then the doorbell rang. At first I refused to believe it. Please God, the noise must be something shaken loose in my ear. But the doorbell rang again and would not stop. I tried not to panic. I took a deep breath, stood up slowly and tottered to the bedroom window, waiting for the sound of footsteps retreating to the street on the stairs outside. But the bell would not stop. I thought it was an angry neighbour. I thought it was the police. I ran back to the bed and pulled the second knife from my Harrods bag. The handle was fat and cold in my hand as I tried to make my fingers grip. Should I cut and slash my way to freedom or stretch out my arm and surrender the blade?

I scuttled to the door, flung it open with a shout and glared into the darkness. A girl was standing on the step. She was wearing a long black dress and nursed a bottle of cheap red wine in her arms. The dress was absurdly decorated with artificial flowers, starched cotton petals stitched in bunches at the throat and wrists. They shook their heads hopelessly whenever she moved.

"Sorry," she said breathlessly, "I've disturbed you."

"What?" I said in a vague manner.

"I've disturbed you," she pointed at the knife clutched feebly in my rubber fist.

"You're cooking." When she smiled she bared her teeth.

I nodded helplessly. The girl walked into the apartment and presented me with the bottle of wine. It was then that she noticed I was wearing a raincoat. She frowned when I closed the door.

"Where's Doris?"

"She's in the bedroom," I said.

"Is she sick?"

"Yes."

The girl walked past me and paused at the bedroom door. She had thin yellow hair and smelled of cinnamon. I swung the bottle and brought it down against her head. Her skull sang with the clarity of a glass bell. The bottle did not break. I threw it across the room and it bounced on the carpet. The girl fell down against the bed. She was moaning and rolling her eyes. The flowers settled in a wreath around her neck. I dragged at the blanket, trying to wrap her into a parcel. It was terrible. She began to struggle and I pulled the blanket tighter against her face. She made a horrible, muffled roar and started to sneeze. When at last she stopped fighting I couldn't tell whether she was alive or dead. She was very quiet. But I was too frightened to unwrap her and inspect the damage.

While I was watching the blanket Doris stood up to leave the room. She paused at the door and squinted at me. She ignored the handle of the knife protruding from her chest. But she kept wiping the naked foot against the carpet as if baffled by the loss of her slipper.

"Where are you going?" I whispered.

"I'm thirsty," she wheezed and shuffled away.

I followed her into the kitchen. She drank a cup of water, laid the cup down on the table, sank to her knees and finally died.

I stared at Doris. I stared at the table. I couldn't believe it. The table had been laid for supper. It was a supper for five people and three of the guests had not yet arrived! I kept counting the chairs that crowded round the little table, counted and counted again, as if by counting I might reduce their number. And then the doorbell rang again.

This time I did not hesitate. I marched to the door. I had made a mess of everything. The evening had been a dreadful mistake. I was a desperate man.

There was a figure in a crumpled suit and a striped green shirt standing outside. He was alone. A huge bottle of cheap red wine was swinging gently in his fist.

"Sorry I'm late," he said cheerfully.

I opened my mouth but no words came out. I felt as limp as Nectarine Summers.

"You look like you've just arrived yourself," he said, nodding at my raincoat.

"What?"

"Are you coming or going?" he demanded.

"I was going to leave."

"Where's Doris?" he said, straining his neck to stare over my shoulder.

"She's in the kitchen," I said. "Can I take your wine?"

"Thanks," he said absently. He pushed the bottle into my hands and stepped inside. He swaggered into the kitchen and stared at Doris on the floor.

"Jesus Christ," he shouted. He did a little tap-dance of horror.

The bottle was very slippery in my rubber fists. I managed to swing it over my head and bring it down against his left ear. The raincoat rattled as the glass bomb exploded. I was covered in droplets of bright red wine and brilliant splinters of glass.

The man in the crumpled suit tumbled against the table. A plate did a somersault in surprise. The table lurched wildly and fell among the chairs. He rolled into the tablecloth and fell on the floor with the cloth wrapped around his head.

When it was finished I hurried into the bedroom, pulled off the raincoat and stuffed it into the Harrods bag. I ran towards the front door, praying that I could reach it before the bell rang again. I burst through the door, clattered up the stone stairs and emerged on the street. No one saw me leave the premises. I peeled off the rubber gloves as I stood there and poked them into the bag. I had escaped. I had escaped.

I wanted to run, run from the wailing sirens and the snarling dogs but the street was empty and I could barely balance on my buckling legs. It was a cool night. I hobbled home through Kilburn, along the Edgware Road, across Marble Arch and down Park Lane. It was a long, punishing walk but every step helped restore my courage and clear my head. When I got home it was still early. I did not want to sleep so I sat down and watched television. A cinema had caught fire in a little French town and killed twenty people.

The following day it was as if the murders had never happened. It was a peculiar flat feeling. I had killed them, yes, but they had not gone for they continued to live in my head. I carried them around with me and it was impossible to believe that they had been removed from the world. There was a dull ache behind my eyes. I felt tired and disappointed, as if I had woken up to discover my lover fled from the bed and nothing left but a shallow grave beside me in the warm sheets. It was finished. The weeks of gleeful speculation and the agony of waiting, the fear and the horror were gone. The brilliant clarity with which I had seen everything had faded into the dull monochrome of another unremarkable morning, so that I might have been emerging from a fantastic dream.

The fever had left me and I half believed that if I dared pay a visit to the Empire Stores I would see Doris miraculously restored and standing behind her counter again.

I washed and shaved and then unpacked the Harrods bag, stuffed overnight in the wardrobe. When I slipped my hand inside the bag it sank to the wrist in a cold, congealed mess of rubber and blood. It was horrible. A filthy tripe that I drew from the bag and threw in the bath. In the excitement of killing I had not seen the blood. The knowledge that I had carried it home from Kilburn made me shiver in disgust. I ran the water and watched the blood and the clothes begin to separate, the blood thinning, the rubber swelling, until the raincoat and the gloves were washed clean. Then I washed the Harrods bag and the bath, the floor beside the bath, the tiles along the wall. It was an hour or more before I finally washed my hands of the whole damned mess.

In the afternoon I walked into the station and bought a newspaper. It was obvious, at a glance, that I had not turned myself into front-page news, an overnight sensation. I felt disappointed. But a careful search uncovered a brief mention of the murders in one of the centre pages. It was just a paragraph but I thought it worth saving. I had worked hard enough for it. So I bought a scrapbook from Woolworth, went home and pasted the clipping into the book.

> "Police are today investigating the deaths of two young women and a man whose bodies were discovered in a Kilburn basement late last night. The police are treating the deaths as murder."

I read the paragraph many times that evening. There was no fear of capture. It was not worth considering the risk. Who would want to force their way into a neglected Kilburn basement and kill the inhabitants? What reason was there for such a curious slaughter? It was senseless. Exactly. The police would chase motives that did not exist. It would drive them crazy. I fried some potatoes and rashers of bacon and ate them in front of the television. They were still digging corpses from the smouldering wreckage of the cinema.

It was a week after the Kilburn killings that Dorothy and Archie appeared again. It was Archie's birthday and Dorothy had persuaded him to spend a few days in London. They phoned me from an hotel in South Kensington but within an hour I had them safely installed in my apartment.

I was happy and flustered by their sudden arrival; we had exchanged a few brief letters since my move to the city but I had not expected to see them. And now here they sat on my sofa, grinning like alligators and complaining about the hotel.

"I hate hotels," said Dorothy. "I can't sleep in their beds. They never give you enough pillows."

I sympathised but scolded them for not warning me of their visit.

"There's no reason to use a hotel – you're always welcome to stay with me. I've got lots of room."

They thanked me kindly and tried to look surprised by the invitation but Archie gave Dorothy a guilty glance and blushed.

"We thought you might have established a little harem for yourself," grinned Dorothy. "It must be lonely here."

"I enjoy the solitude."

"I couldn't live in London," complained Dorothy, "It frightens me."

"It's a violent city," I said.

"That doesn't worry me," grunted Archie as he admired his fists. "If anyone tried to interfere with me I'd skin 'em alive."

I believed him.

"So what do you do with yourself?" persisted Dorothy.

"Oh, I pass the time," I said.

She smiled.

"I couldn't live without my work," said Archie, "Some men are born to be butchers."

"I hate it," said Dorothy, "Your clothes smell of blood." She shivered at the thought and smoothed her skirt against her knees.

"Blood thickens gravy," sighed Archie serenely.

During the following days we made a grand tour of the city. We took a boat along the Thames and counted the bridges. Dorothy stood with her face turned into the wind, staring along the Embankment while Archie sprawled over the side of the boat, trailing his hands in the purple water.

"They find a hundred bodies in the Thames every year," I told him.

Archie looked impressed. He pulled his hand from the water and sniffed his fingers.

"They're mostly accidents and suicides," I added wistfully.

The next day we took a bus to the Zoo and considered the giraffes. Archie told me he had once met a man who had tasted giraffe meat but Dorothy said it wasn't true. On the third day she demanded to be shown the museums in Exhibition Road and spent hours peering at prehistoric bones. But Archie grew bored and complained, so we left to inspect the meat in Harrod's Food Hall. He carried an Instamatic on a cord around his neck and had a curious way of holding it briefly against his eye and then dropping it again as if he were squinting at the world through a monocle. He took several pictures of the salmon in the mermaid's grotto but was not impressed by the sight of the sausage and ham. When he was finished we cut through Knightsbridge Green and walked down Rotten Row to Hyde Park Corner where we risked our lives to reach Green Park.

The last time I had seen Dorothy she had been careful to maintain a little distance between us but now, as we kicked through the leaves towards Buckingham Palace, she took hold of my arm and clung to it gleefully.

I smiled at myself, amazed. It was hard to believe that this mild and happy man was the same creature who had spent the previous week on his hands and knees peering with murderous intent into some grubby basement. It had been nothing but a bad dream, a nocturnal raving, and now the grey afternoon light dissipated its force and left me doubting that it had ever happened. While Dorothy clung to my arm I could not remember what strange appetite had possessed me to murder but I was resolved that it should not possess me again. I was free and I was content. I had performed the most dangerous of all conjuring tricks and it would be foolish to risk another performance. It was finished. Yet, at the same time, it remained difficult to imagine that Doris Forest was altogether dead for she continued to inhabit some dark corner of my head and lived there in rude good health.

We reached home that evening exhausted. They had arranged to leave the following day and reluctantly began to pack their luggage. But despite everything Dorothy had not quite finished celebrating Archie's birthday. While he sat slumped in a chair she produced a bottle of champagne and a sheaf of smoked salmon and laid out a picnic on the carpet at his feet. I found brandy for the champagne, brown bread for the salmon, and we feasted and talked together.

"You should get married," declared Archie as he gulped at his champagne. "London must be full of girls who would appreciate a bright young sprat like you."

"A city can be a very lonely place," corrected Dorothy. "It's not easy to make friends."

"I'm sure Mackerel doesn't have any trouble," said the butcher.

Dorothy wrapped a shred of smoked salmon around her finger and poked it into her mouth. She glanced across at me, waiting for me to make some reply.

"I've made one or two friends," I said. "It doesn't bother me."

"Exactly," boomed the butcher cheerfully. "Fill up your bed and keep out the draughts. That's my advice. You'll be married before you know it. And then it's too late."

"Archie," scolded Dorothy, "You make marriage sound like a prison sentence."

"Don't misunderstand me. I'm a happy man. I believe in marriage. That's why I'm trying to persuade Mackerel to find himself a good woman."

Dorothy was not satisfied with his explanation. "You're trying to persuade him to sleep with everyone he meets," she said as she filled his glass.

"Well, you have to look around. I'm lucky. We're happy. But he'll have to go a long way to find someone like you," he crooned.

It was past midnight when we finally hauled ourselves to our beds.

But I had hardly managed to pull on my pyjamas when there was a faint scratching at the door. When I went to investigate the noise I found Dorothy standing outside my room. She was wearing a dressing-gown of post-card blue silk.

"Can I get you anything?" I whispered.

Dorothy smiled. "No, I just wanted to come and say goodnight." She stepped into the room and looked around.

"Where's Archie?" I whispered, pulling my pyjamas together with a casual brush of my hand.

"Asleep."

"I'm sorry you're leaving tomorrow," I said as I followed her across the room.

"Are you, Mackerel?" she asked, turning around and staring at me for a moment.

"Yes," I said and frowned.

"Do you remember the time when you stayed with your aunt and we played together?"

"Yes," I said, "I remember that time."

"And do you remember the game?"

"I haven't forgotten," I said softly.

She had washed away her make-up and the greyhound had returned to her face. The mouth was dark and when she smiled she bared her sharp little teeth. She was standing too close to me and I stepped back nervously.

"You have such lovely eyes," she said gently.

"Thank you."

"They're such a beautiful colour – like stained emeralds," she continued. She was standing so close against me I could feel the warmth of her skin through her dressing-gown.

"Thank you," I whispered again.

"It's the first thing I noticed about you when we met for the first time. Those big, gentle eyes," she murmured as she stared into my face. Her breath smelt of toothpaste and came in short, warm gusts.

"What will happen if Archie wakes up and finds us together?" I asked nervously.

"Don't worry. He won't wake up. I've given him a sleeping tablet."

"What?"

"Yes, I've got hundreds of them," she said carelessly. "All different shapes and sizes."

"Show me," I said.

She slipped into the bathroom and returned with a washbag full of bottles of sleeping tablets. She poked her fingers into the bag, rattling the bottles together.

"Isn't it dangerous?" I enquired.

"No, I do it all the time," she scoffed.

"Why?"

"Oh, he gets difficult sometimes," she sighed and laid down the bag beside the bed.

I was desperate to know what kind of difficulties Dorothy experienced at the hands of the butcher, but I was too shy to ask the question.

There was a heavy silence. It was the kind of silence in which a woman waits, patiently, stubbornly, for something to happen. I understood the signal but I didn't know what to do about it.

The old wardrobe contained the full sexual history of William Mackerel Burton. My brief assault on Figg had taught me nothing and, since that time, I had devoted myself and all my energies to learning my craft. I might fall to the floor and feign death but I suspected that Dorothy was expecting more of me than a warm corpse. I knew the basic attitudes and gestures that lovers are expected to assume, of course, but I didn't know where to begin.

I stared at Dorothy with a pale grin. For a few moments I vacillated between sweeping her into my arms and brushing her out of the room. Then I reached forward to kiss her mouth.

"No," she whispered and turned her face away.

"What do you want?" I asked in dismay.

She plucked the belt from the dressing-gown and thrust it silently into my hand. Then she stepped from the gown and let it slither to her feet.

She had legs of the most remarkable length, as if she had been engineered for sprinting great distances over difficult terrain. Barefoot, she stood on tiptoe with her calves flexed and the bones of her ankles drawn tight. Her hips were narrow and sharp. The hair between her legs had been shaved to stubble.

She raised her hands and gently rubbed the cones of her breasts. Her fingers had been stripped of their rings. She held out her hands towards me.

"Here. Tie my wrists together," she commanded.

"Why?"

"Don't keep asking silly questions, Mackerel. Play the game. Come on, tie me up."

I bandaged her wrists with the cord and secured them with an elaborate knot. Dorothy inspected my work carefully and nodded her approval. She sat down on the edge of the bed.

"Feet," she whispered.

I was beginning to get the idea. I scampered about the room searching for shackles. I found a scarf, a leather belt and a long elastic strap. I arranged my equipment on the pillow. Then I tied her ankles together. I threaded the elastic strap around her knees, drew her knees beneath her chin and buckled the strap behind her neck. I used the belt to secure her wrists around her knees. As I worked she muttered little encouragements to me, gasped when I tightened and tested my knots.

"Does it hurt?" I whispered doubtfully.

"No," she gasped. "Tie me tighter – use your strength."

I wrenched at the knot until the leather burned my fingers.

"Does *that* hurt?" I whispered in a hoarse voice.

"No," she squeaked, "It doesn't hurt."

When I was finished she was rolled into a tight bundle and I stepped back to admire my work. And then I noticed that her eyes were closed and her mouth was open, exposing her teeth. I was afraid she had fainted. I peered anxiously into her face and she surprised me with a kiss, stabbed my mouth sharply with the stiffness of her tongue.

I made an urgent search for a way into a closer embrace. But there was none to be found. No matter how I rolled her about the floor I could not force an entry. Her breasts were pushed flat against her knees. Her feet were knotted together and the heels pressed securely against the stubble between her thighs. I was in a lather of lust but there was nothing I could do to prise her apart. It was very frustrating.

I struggled to embrace her for a long time until, weary with the game, she woke up and wriggled from bondage, slippery as Houdini. She wriggled and kicked and the knots exploded from her ankles and wrists. She stood up and grinned at me.

"Lie down on the bed, Mackerel," she said as she gathered up the shackles.

I clambered aboard and lay down, adjusting the pillow behind my head and trying to hide the excitement in my pyjamas with my hands.

"Relax," she whispered soothingly, "Stretch out your legs and close your eyes."

"What are you doing?" I panted as I thrust out my feet and screwed up my face.

"Are you frightened?" she asked.

"No."

"Do you trust me?"

"Yes."

She took the leather belt and shook it, making it crack like a whip. As she bent to tie my wrists, she touched my face with the tips of her breasts. She pulled my wrists above my head and buckled the belt around my neck.

"Does it hurt?" she inquired sympathetically.

"No," I said. It was very uncomfortable, but I was too excited to complain.

She crawled onto the bed and sat astride me, wrapping my

legs in the long elastic strap. She worked quickly and in silence, threading the strap around my knees and wrenching at the knots to pull them tight. She was not satisfied until I was helpless.

"We're a couple of outlaws," she whispered as she stood above me and blew me a kiss. Her eyes were very bright and her face was hot.

"Goodnight." And she tiptoed safely back to Archie. It took me until dawn to escape. She was a natural villain.

Dorothy and Archie left before breakfast. It began to rain. The streets were slippery and black. Office girls huddled in doorways and stamped their feet. Old men clung to their umbrellas and were blown beneath buses. Pigeons tried to shelter in drains and were drowned. The Thames was a boiling mustard. The dark sky sagged around the glittering peaks of Victoria Station.

I watched television for two or three days, asleep with my eyes open. I felt lethargic and bored. The apartment was empty without Dorothy and nothing pleased me. I sprawled on the sofa and watched television, without moving, without blinking, until my eyes burned and my brains were scorched. Finally, more dead than alive, I managed to crawl away, throw a towel over its enormous, glaring eye and tear the plug from the wall. I stood up and yawned in the silence. The rain stopped blistering the windows. It was time to pull myself together and resist the monotonous winter twilight. So I painted the kitchen and forced myself to take morning walks in the park. I took driving lessons and began to collect books. My days were stitched together again by little repetitions and rituals.

I bought parcels of books from a charity shop and read whatever I happened to find. There were romances, Westerns, thrillers and mysteries, hymn books, travel books, gardening books and scrap books. The books were mostly mildewed. But I was happy to read everything. And in one of these books I found the Dusseldorf Vampire.

The vampire's name was Peter Kurten and he killed for

pleasure. He killed women and drank their blood. He killed men and children and dogs and horses. He was bewitched by the smell of hot blood. He was amazed by its colour and drugged by its perfume. He killed in sexual ecstasy. He killed in hypnotised delight. When he could not kill he set buildings ablaze because the ripening flames reminded him of spurting arteries.

During the day the Vampire was a mild and ordinary man. There was a photograph of him in the book. He might have been a tailor or perhaps sold life insurance. His shirts were starched and his hair combed. But at night, while his wife worked, he went hunting in the frightened streets. He was a mad old tiger. He killed but the slaughter only sharpened his hunger to kill again.

The Vampire was caught in 1931 and executed in Cologne. He was afraid of the guillotine. He was afraid the blade might be so swift he would have no time to smell his own blood.

I read the book and then I read it a second time. I understood the Vampire, the danger and excitement of his addiction. It did not shock me. The vampire dwells in every man. It is only fear that prevents us feasting on forbidden pleasures. What sweet, unspeakable terrors startle us awake at night, sweating and aroused? What shadows drift in our eyes as we stand to stare at accidents in the street, straining towards the stain of blood? The vampire sleeps in every man yet only the few dare to share its flight. The Dusseldorf Vampire gorged on blood where others are afraid to press their lips. But I understood the Vampire. I shared his addiction. I was most alive when I killed.

Oh yes, it was true that I missed Dorothy's mischief and the rain certainly depressed me; but I ached most deeply for the smell of blood. I craved for that most powerful narcotic and the Vampire's story made me anxious to capture that thrill again. It would be easier and swifter the next time I made a killing because I was determined to learn from my mistakes. I had been no more than lucky in Kilburn but in the future I would be sharp and sudden and very clean.

My first task then was to find a suitable sacrifice. There had been a lot of wasted energy searching for Doris. Death, after all, does not pick and choose his victims so carefully. He strikes at random. So I packed my shopping bag one evening and went out in search of murder.

There are many ways to kill a man but I have always favoured the knife. Knives are silent and precise. A pistol will kill at arm's length but I do not trust them. Chung Ling Soo, the celestial Chinese conjurer, was killed on the stage of the Wood Green Empire while attempting to catch a rifle bullet in his hand. I packed a pair of filleting knives, my raincoat and gloves and a Polaroid camera. Archie's Instamatic had given me a new interest in photography.

The night was dry but cold enough to keep tourists off the streets. I took a bus from the station, rode as far as Piccadilly Circus and walked into Soho and beyond. I cannot say exactly where I walked because I was soon lost but it was a miserable corner of the city. The streets trickled into alleys and the buildings were shuttered or abandoned. I turned this corner and that corner, working myself deeper into the maze, until I reached a narrow alley of broken cobbles. The alley was in darkness but for a red light that shone from a room above a derelict restaurant.

I laid down my bag and looked around me. The alley seemed to end in a high brick wall and the surrounding buildings were either empty or locked. I was especially interested in the rubble that had once been the Queen of India and finally, through a mouldering archway, I found a flight of stone stairs that seemed to lead directly to the rooms above the shell of the restaurant. In the shelter of the arch, pinned to the crumbling plaster, someone had pinned a little cardboard sign, 1st Floor Patsy.

I pulled on my raincoat and gloves, climbed the stairs and found myself in a dirty corridor confronting two identical doors. I hammered on the first of the doors with my fist. An old man opened it and peered out, searching for me in the gloom. Across his shoulder I glimpsed a small, untidy room, hot and stinking, with a television blaring on a table.

Without waiting for an invitation I pushed the old man

backwards into the room and closed the door behind me. The old man looked startled but did not complain. He was wearing a shapeless blue suit and a pair of broken carpet slippers that made him walk with a shuffle. He sat down in a chair and turned his face towards the television. He seemed resigned to receiving unwelcome guests.

"You've come to the wrong place," he shouted at me.

"No," I said, "I don't think I've made a mistake."

"Yes," he shouted above the noise of the television. "Yes. The bitch works next door. She's next door." He gestured with his thumb towards the wall.

"Is she there tonight?" I asked.

"She's always there. She never stops," he shouted, "Thumpty, thumpty, thump. Day and night. She'll kill herself one day. Bitch." He pulled a tobacco tin from his pocket and began to make himself a cigarette, taking a pinch of tobacco and rolling it in the palm of his hand. His face was absurdly crumpled. His eyes were pools of bright water, almost hidden among the folds and creases. He rolled the cigarette idly between his fingers. He was waiting for me to realise my mistake and leave him alone. He was expecting me to creep next door to Patsy.

But as I looked around the room at the remains of this old man's life I knew I had business with him.

"This used to be a good area," he grumbled, "You could walk the streets in safety."

"It's all changing," I said.

"It's full of tarts," he muttered as he poked his pockets for a box of matches. "Tarts and their darkie boyfriends."

"They shouldn't be allowed on the streets," I agreed.

"I was in the war," he said as he struck a match and sucked at the cigarette, "I fought against foreigners. And now they're everywhere. This used to be a good area when I was a young man. You could walk the streets . . ."

I took a knife from my bag and reached out towards the old neck. As he felt death approach he turned to confront me. I tried to make a grab at him but he jerked back and fell off his chair. He hit the floor and his teeth fell out. He sat up and covered his mouth in his hands. He was just a bundle of rags and bones. His teeth sat beside him on the carpet.

I bent down and caught hold of his collar. He began to shout and thrash around with his arms. But I was too strong for him, placed the tip of the blade at the base of his ear and drove it smoothly into his brain. It was like forcing a knife through a pineapple. But he didn't bleed. Perhaps it was the angle of the knife or the shape of the blade that plugged the wound. There was not enough blood to fill a saucer. I stood up, trembling, and stared at the corpse. I was filled with horror and delight.

How can I make you understand the beauty of the ravishing blade? How can I make you understand when you cling so anxiously to the hovel you fondly call your body? I come in the night to cut you loose from your skin and bone and set you free to drift, invisible and safe from war, poverty and disease. It is done in a moment. The squirming, wriggling dance of death. The sweet hot perfume of rubber and blood. Open your arms and embrace me.

I hammered on the second door and a woman's voice shouted back at me. I could not understand what she shouted. So I continued to hammer until the door opened with a flourish of chains.

She wasn't very old but her face had already hardened into an expression of bored belligerence. Life had made her sneer so often that her lips had grown curly and pulled out of shape. There was a fine blue scar across the bridge of her nose. Her eyes were pink and her short, black hair was smeared damply around her ears. They were very small ears and had to work hard to carry the weight of an enormous pair of glass earrings shaped like pears. When she moved her head the pears swung back and forth against her jaw. She was wearing something that looked like a shower curtain trimmed with feathers. She peered at me standing there in my raincoat and gloves and called me a filthy word.

"Excuse me?"

"I don't do anything nasty," she sneered, pulling at my raincoat with her fingers.

"What?"

"You're sick," she said, "You need a doctor."

"But I saw your advertisement downstairs . . ."

"You made a mistake. Try next door," she said with a jerk of her head. She was wearing a strong perfume that wafted through the shower curtain whenever she made the slightest movement. It was a queer, sweet animal smell – the scent of baboons eating wedding cake.

"I've already tried next door," I smiled. The shower curtain had fallen open.

"So try again tomorrow night," she sighed impatiently.

"It won't take long," I said.

She drew the curtain tighter and the feathers trembled at her throat.

"I happen to be entertaining an important international businessman," she said, "And if you don't piss off he'll probably come out and break both your legs."

Then she tried to close the door in my face.

"Oh, but I'm interested in violence of every description," I crooned as I broke into the room and slammed the door.

The room was filled by a muddy red light. It stained the walls to the colour of brickdust. The pasteboard furniture glowed dark as claret. The very air seemed rouged. But even the flattering nature of the light could do nothing to improve the appearance of the brute who sat on the bed and glared at me.

He was huge. He was wearing nothing but a pair of purple underpants and he sat on the bed like an ugly Buddha, nipples the size of raspberries, scratching the hair on his massive belly. When he glowered at me he looked angry, but he also looked frightened, and began to cradle himself in his arms as if he felt cold.

"What's your game?" he barked at Patsy. "Who is this clown?"

"Jesus, I don't know."

"You've got the wrong address, my friend," he growled at me. "You'll find the door behind you. Don't fall down the stairs."

"No, this is what I want," I said cheerfully and laid down my bag at the foot of the bed.

"Piss off!" screeched 1st Floor Patsy. "I'm working . . ."

I stared at the man in his underpants. The hair on his head was thin, grey and grown very long against his neck. He began to stroke it nervously.

"We were just having a few drinks," he said in a defensive tone of voice.

Patsy kept glancing at the telephone. I walked forward, picked up the telephone and tore the cable from its socket. I had seen it many times on television; the killer bursts into the room and finds the kidnapped girl trying to phone for help. He slaps the girl to the floor and whips the cable from the wall like licorice bootlace. The girl screams. The killer grins and shapes the bootlace into a noose. But it's not so easy. I wrenched at the cable but it would not leave its anchor. I wrapped it around my fist and pulled against the wall with all my weight but the cable seemed to stretch to impossible lengths. Finally it snapped and threw me against the bed.

"Stop him, Jumbo," screeched Patsy.

The man stood up and then sat down again at the sight of the knife.

"What do you want?" asked Jumbo.

"I've come to collect you,"

"Nobody knows I'm here. My wife is . . ."

"I've come to collect your souls," I said grandly.

"You're mad," declared Patsy, "What are you going to do with us? What do you want?"

"I'm going to kill you."

"You can't kill me – you don't know me," blurted Jumbo.

"I don't like the look of you."

"What kind of reason is that for killing someone?"

"It's enough of a reason. Thousands of people are killed every year because they're the wrong colour or have the wrong opinions. You're nothing special. You happen to be in the wrong place at the wrong time."

"Calm down, my friend," said Jumbo nervously, "You'll find my wallet over there in my jacket. If you need money, take whatever you want – but don't hurt me."

"I want to take some pictures," I said. I reached into my bag and pulled out the Polaroid.

"Yes," said Patsy with enthusiasm, "Yes, that's better – let's have some fun."

Jumbo smiled, stood up and began to search for his clothes, scattered on the carpet around the bed. He thought he was going home.

"Sit down," I shouted at him, "Sit down or I'll cut your ears off."

He jumped back to the safety of the bed and pressed his hands between his legs as if his fingers were scalded.

"Now tie him up," I told Patsy and shook the knife in my fist.

"I told you already I don't do any of that stuff," she shouted back defiantly.

"Use your imagination," pleaded Jumbo, who was afraid for his ears.

Patsy glared at him and plucked some towels from the back of a chair. She began to tie the Buddha by his hands and feet.

"Yes, that's very good," I said as I watched her working the knots.

"What do you want me to do now?" she hissed at me when she was finished.

"Smile," I said cheerfully, "Sit on his lap and smile."

She perched herself carefully on Jumbo's broad knees and watched nervously while I fiddled with the Polaroid. When I raised the camera to my eye they both began to smile as if their lives depended on it. They peeled back their faces and bared their teeth. Patsy pulled back the shower curtain to display her legs and wrapped her arms around Jumbo's neck. I took a couple of pictures and laid them on the table to develop and dry.

It was while I was putting the camera back in my bag that Patsy slipped off Jumbo and crept towards me. I turned to confront her with the knife but she dropped to her knees and tried to lift the hem of my raincoat.

"Let's play another game," she crooned as she fumbled

with the buttons of my trousers. She was hoping to escape the hard edge of the knife and cheat death by accepting the thrusts of my soft and porky dagger.

"No," I cried in alarm and pushed her away. I was shocked. "I haven't finished."

Patsy stood up and began to walk backwards across the room. She must have smelt the violence in me. She said nothing.

"What are you going to do with that knife?" whimpered Jumbo as I moved towards him.

"Don't be alarmed," I said gently.

"I have important friends," he threatened as he struggled to shake loose the towels.

"Congratulations," I said.

"Please, please don't hurt me," he begged as I stroked his ear with the tip of the blade.

"Oh, it shouldn't hurt," I reassured him. The knife was already deep in his neck. I gave it a twist and turned it towards his brains. He seemed to rise from the bed, float for a moment in mid-air and then somersault gracefully across the carpet where he settled in an ugly heap.

"Oh, my God, you've killed me!" he gasped, "You've gone and fucking killed me."

I turned to Patsy. She was standing with her hands pressed hard against the wall, staring down at the corpse in horror. Her face was green. She took several steps towards the fallen Jumbo and fainted. She fell in a flurry of feathers with her arms thrown over her face. I was grateful for her assistance. I am not a squeamish man but there was something about Patsy that made me hesitate with the knife. I could not risk letting her stay alive but, at the same time, I did not relish helping her into the land of the dead. Her faint would serve as an anaesthetic. While she was still insensible I found a fruit knife and tucked it quickly behind her ear.

I have no regrets. A dozen or more people pushed in or out of the world makes no difference in the grand balance of the universe. They are grains of sand. Every day a hundred children die in Africa from starvation, a hundred more choke to death on their milkshakes in the USA, a thousand more are born in China. It's not a question of justice. No one selects them, one from another. Death, in all his wonderful variety, is deaf to prayers and blind to blessings.

You may call me a butcher but electric toasters kill more people in a year than I could manage to touch in a lifetime. There are men who are actually *paid* to deal in death. Men with good educations and respectable families. Point your finger in their direction. They walk into the office each morning and get paid to dream of new, exciting ways to destroy the world. They make careers from it. Listen, I've got a good idea; why don't we seed the clouds and make it rain acid over the cities? No that's too expensive. But if we poison the water we could make the women barren and turn their bones to chalk. Yes, that's better and we could probably do it within the budget. But it's too slow. What we want is wind, fire and a damned big bang. Let's have some lunch and think about radiation sickness.

I frighten you because I work on a human scale, bring you death as a personal gift, an intimate melodrama for your parlour. But there are nightmares in the world so grand that your head could not contain them.

What was I talking about? Ah, yes, I had just plugged Patsy's ear with a knife. There is an extraordinary silence that descends upon the dead. One moment they had been struggling to stay alive, their blood rippling beneath their skins, hair erect, eyes wild, their mouths spurting nonsense. The next moment they were as motionless as furniture. They might have been torn mattresses, tightly rolled and thrown on the floor. I considered taking a final Polaroid but decided against it. I packed up my equipment and left the premises.

As soon as I had reached the safety of my little lair I unpacked my bag and scrubbed down the raincoat and gloves in the bath. There was less blood than I had imagined but it is important to remain clean. I placed the precious photographs on the bedside table, ready for inspection at my leisure, and then settled in front of the TV to dry and dust my faithful rubber gloves. A delicious fatigue settled over me and I was almost asleep when there was a tapping on the door.

When I answered it I found Johnson Johnson standing there in his carpet slippers, grinning and forking his fingers through the remains of his hair.

"What's the trouble?" I asked nervously.

"Good evening, Mr Burton," he smiled, staring over my shoulder and stretching his neck to peer into my room. "We heard you come home."

"I went for a walk," I blurted and then felt annoyed with myself for feeling that I had to explain anything to the wretched Johnson Johnson.

"You should be careful," he said, "The streets are dangerous at night."

"I'm old enough to take care of myself."

"No one is safe," he said with a wag of his head.

"Is there anything else?" I demanded impatiently.

"I wonder if you would care to turn down your television? My mother, you understand, has a crippling headache and she can't sleep through the noise. I'm sorry to disturb you."

I was taken by surprise. I mumbled some apology and began to close the door. But Johnson Johnson had not finished.

"I hope," he continued slowly and with a fading smile, "I hope you won't be doing any housework at this time of night."

"Housework?" I whispered, perplexed by his concern. Was this some kind of old maid's joke? "What housework?"

He noddeed at the rubber gloves that I clutched in my fist. I was so shocked I could find no reply and he smirked as if he had caught me trying to stuff an inflatable woman down the front of my pants. I began screwing the gloves into a ball but they wriggled loose and sprang into the air. Johnson Johnson bent down and picked the gloves from the floor. As he returned them he looked at me sharply with his bright, cunning eyes.

"I'm sorry to disturb you," he said again, and there was something in his tone of voice that made my blood run cold.

*

I never went walking again. I bought a little Volkswagen. It was old, scratched and a muddy shade of red but I did not want anything ostentatious. The engine was reliable and strong – that was important. I paid particular attention to the details of tax, insurance and parking permits: in my kind of work you cannot afford to be careless. And, when everything was in order, I took to the road. It made sweet changes in my life. Sometimes, when I felt restless, I cruised through the city and watched the crowds. At night I could park in the quiet streets of Swiss Cottage and Camden Town and sit in the darkness, watching the lights of the surrounding houses. Sitting so snug with the rain lashing at the windscreen I fancied, as I stared into brightly-lit kitchens and parlours, that I was contained in a bathysphere and peering at life on the ocean floor. The Volkswagen was a sealed chamber from which I could make my observations in safety and comfort. No one seemed to notice me sitting motionless behind the wheel and, as a precaution, I liked to keep a map on my knees so that, if I were ever challenged by the police, I could claim to be lost and ask directions.

I took delight in the knowledge that this most innocuous machine with its battered bonnet and faded paintwork was destined to become the transport of death. It was such an unlikely disguise. When, in your dreams, has death sprung upon you from a secondhand Volkswagen?

It was November and I had no plans to kill again that year. I remained intoxicated by the memory of Patsy and the wretched Jumbo. In the smallness of the night, I referred to my precious Polaroids and, staring at them, found I could recollect everything in the most vivid and intimate detail. Those two photographs unlocked a macabre peepshow which kept me hot and excited through many wintry nights.

It was during the worst of the weather that I made a friend of my neighbour, Frank Plimsoll, the American who lived beneath Johnson Johnson. He owned a set of rooms cluttered with books and bric-a-brac and had spent most of his life trying to force the rudiments of world history into the stubborn skulls of schoolboys. He had lived in London for several years and had connections with a school in Chelsea. I cannot remember our first conversation but we would nod and smile at each other when we passed on the stairs and eventually grew familiar enough to spend evenings together exchanging books and opinions on the world.

I could not guess at his age but he was certainly twenty years or more my senior. He had soft brown hair and a big, crinkled face. He liked to wear corduroy suits and heavy brogues which gave the impression of a gamekeeper dressed for church. He was slow and affable and generally in search of a woman.

You must understand, he was not a man in search of a wife. Indeed, Frank seemed to live in dread of being trapped into any kind of emotional dependence upon a woman. No, he enjoyed fucking strangers. It was a sport. He liked to rent women for the night and had travelled around the world in search of novelties and bargains. He seemed to have a good, general knowledge of most of the brothels in the world. He had used brothels and bawdy houses like other people used hotels, moving from one to another as he travelled around. He said there were brothels in Bombay where the women were kept in bamboo cages overlooking the streets. He said there were bars in West Africa where a woman could be bought for a bottle of Guinness and a few cigarettes. He was an education. He spoke of his experiences in foreign parts as if he were describing nothing more remarkable than the local food and wine. There was never anything cheap or sensational about his stories. His adventures somehow managed to sound like something from *National Geographic*.

Everything he told me about the world was fascinating. He was the first man who had spoken to me about the carnal pursuits and I was very impressed. Naturally these conversations would have been impossible with my mother or my aunt, Figg or even Dorothy and I did not yet trust Archie enough to approach him on such delicate aspects of human nature. Frank was like an older, more experienced brother and I was flattered, I suppose, that he took it for granted that I should be made fully acquainted with the sensual pleasures of the world.

We spent several evenings in the month before Christmas drinking and talking together. He asked me very few questions about myself but when he asked me how I earned my living I told him I was writing a book on conjurers, a history of conjurers and their illusions. I don't know why. It was the first idea that came into my head. But he seemed perfectly happy with the explanation and encouraged me to furnish the invention with such detail that I almost believed I was writing it. He wanted to see the chapters I had written and I had to make excuses. But I promised that he should be the first to read the finished work.

"I once saw a man in New York who cut a woman into six parts. He locked her in a coffin and attacked it with a chain saw. It was incredible. One of the best tricks I think I've ever seen in my life," he said with considerable enthusiasm.

"How did he do it?" I asked.

"Well, you should know better than to ask such questions. A good magician never betrays his secrets – it would spoil the fun," he chuckled.

"Did you like New York?" I enquired. He rarely spoke about his home.

"I loved it," he sighed.

"Why did you leave?"

"It's too damned violent. Do you know the most common fatal disease among the young men in New York?"

"No," I said and shook my head.

"Murder."

"I don't understand," I said with a shudder.

"Murder. In New York you stand a better chance of being murdered than having a heart attack."

"That's very hard to believe," I said.

He shrugged. "I read it in the *Sunday Times*," he said. He paused then to empty his ashtray. He chain smoked Camels, lit one from the stump of another, hour after hour, so that his rooms were constantly filled by a grey and poisonous fog that stung my eyes and made me cough. His carpets were filled with the soft white ash. His fingers were orange.

"London can be dangerous," I said when he was settled again with the ashtray balanced on his knees.

"Yes," he agreed, "It's not safe any more."

"People are robbed in broad daylight. Old ladies smacked on the head and their handbags snatched . . ."

"It's one of the hazards of life in the city," shrugged Frank. "You learn to live with it."

"Yes, it's like those murders a few weeks ago in Soho," I ventured carelessly. "Fifteen years ago they would have created a sensation – the newspapers would have been boiling for weeks. Now they're accepted as just another bad night."

"Ah, yes, but those murders are different," smiled Frank and paused dramatically to suck on his Camel.

"Different?" I demanded.

"Yes, there's something peculiar about those killings. I think there'll be a few more of them before he's caught."

"Why?"

"He's dangerous," explained Frank. "He's a man who kills purely for pleasure."

"He probably killed for money," I suggested. But Frank shook his head. "According to the papers nothing was stolen. He's a man who murders for sport. And that kind of sport becomes an addiction."

I nodded sagely, "Blood sport," I said.

"Blood sport," he replied.

The rest of our conversation that night is lost to me. He continued to talk and smoke and dream of distant brothels but I remember none of it. He had called me an addict. I couldn't believe it.

But Frank's observations had startled me and I resolved not to make another kill for at least six months or perhaps a year. I was an artist and not driven by the mad desires of an addict. I wanted to prove Frank wrong. And yet, despite myself, I obliged him a few days later by killing again. I could not help myself.

It was a mild night, black as the grave but warm and smelling of rain. I was driving towards Swiss Cottage with my equipment in a bag beside me on the seat. I had not planned a killing but knowing I had the knives with me gave my journey an added touch of excitement. It was thrilling to glance across at the big green Harrods bag and to know that it contained everything I needed to extract the life from whoever I might encounter in the dark.

When I grew tired of driving I parked the car in a quiet street and settled down to watch the lights in the surrounding houses. I had planned nothing. I was happy enough to sit and dream. But around the corner trotted a short fat man in a brown coat. He was followed by a short and very angry woman who was puffing and blowing and clutching at his sleeve. Every few yards he stopped walking and tried to tear his sleeve free from her grasp by slapping her face but she held tight and tried to bite him. Gradually they fought their way to one of the neighbouring houses. There was no light in any of the windows. The man stopped at the front door and fumbled for keys in his pocket. The woman beside him wiped the hair from her face. She raised one knee and used it to balance her handbag while she poked around inside it and produced her own key. Then the man tried to snatch the key from her hand but she pushed him away with her elbow and searched for the lock.

I pulled on my gloves, picked up my knives and glided from the car. When they opened the door I was standing behind them. I followed them into the empty house and the woman had switched on the light before they saw me standing between them.

The man was very drunk and his eyes were as cloudy as poisoned oysters. There were fine red scratches across one cheek, from the ear to the chin, and his mouth looked swollen. He stared and wagged a finger at me as he tried to find the strength to speak. He threatened me with his finger. The woman was almost as drunk as the man. Her lipstick was smudged and bled from the corners of her mouth. Her hair was tangled and her knuckles were bruised. She was wearing a cheap red frock and a small fur jacket. The jacket might have been sewn from cats.

"Who are you, shit-face?" the man finally blurted at me. He sounded as if he had been approached by strange men all evening and I was only one of a crowd who needed introductions. "Is he *another* of your friends?" he shouted at his companion.

The woman said nothing. She was scowling and stroking her cats.

"Get out and take her with you!" he shouted and stumbled towards the door. He made a grab at the woman as he moved but missed by several inches and lost his balance. He spun on his heel and hit the floor. He sat up painfully and rubbed his head.

I knelt down beside him and studied the side of his skull, searching for the place to insert the knife.

"The fucker's got a knife," he burbled gleefully to the woman, as if his worst suspicions about her friends had just been confirmed.

"Look at that, the fucker's got a knife," He pointed at me again with a crooked finger.

His head was swinging loosely from side to side. I cradled the back of his head in one hand and held it firmly while I raised the knife to his ear.

"I'm warning you," he shouted at the woman, "If you don't send your boyfriend home I'm going to kill him."

The tip of the blade had disappeared inside his head. I paused and tightened my grip on the handle, correcting the angle of ascent.

"I could kill you with my bare hands," he sighed. "I was in the army." He struck me in the face with his fist. The fist was soft and damp. It rolled down my face and dropped to the floor. I turned the knife and guided it into the roof of his skull.

The woman was sitting on the stairs with her handbag swinging gently between her knees. She smiled and snivelled and shook her head at the corpse. I took a second knife and approached her gently. I thought, she will take fright and try to clamber up the stairs. I will catch her by the ankles and pull her into my poisoned embrace. But she didn't move. I sat down beside her and took away her handbag. She didn't struggle or scream but merely screwed up her face and turned to the wall. Her hair parted to expose her ear.

"Does it hurt?" she whispered.

"No, it doesn't hurt," I promised.

"I'm very tired," she said sadly.

"Close your eyes," I murmured, "Close your eyes and you'll soon be asleep.

I touched her ear with the knife and she was gone. It wasn't fit to be called a murder. It was more like a suicide. Ten thousand people try to kill themselves every month: a few of them, I suppose, are successful. But most of them make a mess of it, fail to cut deep enough or stay asleep long enough to make it work. They are amateurs. They are dragged into hospitals and washed down and the following month they try it again. It seems such a terrible waste. If they could only reach me, if they only knew my telephone number, I could help them put an end to themselves. There are so many brave volunteers in search of death's door and with a simple turn of the key I could throw it open to them. It would be a pleasure to offer my services. I am fast and I am lethal. I am a master magician. The depressed and suicidal would run to embrace me. If only they knew they had such a friend.

I sat on the stairs and looked at the woman with the knife in her ear. It was a pity I had left the Polaroid at home. She made a lovely picture. Her jacket was spread beneath her like a blanket. The blood burned bright as embers against her skin. I turned out the lights before I left the house and closed the door behind me. It was all over in six or seven minutes.

I stood for a time and sucked in the cold night air, peeling off my rubber gloves as I watched the street. The houses were narrow brick boxes, sheltered by hedges of holly and laurel. Here and there a feeble light seeped through the curtains at a bedroom window. I watched the windows and I thought, in every house, in every bed, there are men and women who lie like corpses as they surrender to sleep. When they wake tomorrow they will count themselves and find that two of their number are gone. And, in that moment, I felt huge as an angel watching over the slumbering world.

As I strolled towards the car I saw an old man with a black dog walking towards me. But only the dog looked in my direction. I drove home, took a hot bath and settled down in front of the television. I was in time, I remember, for the late news. They had just caught the Liverpool Leopard and there was an interview with the chief of police. The Leopard had been running loose for over two years, raping women and stealing their clothes. There was a picture of him. He was a mild young man with a spotty face and a neat moustache. It was strange to think of him rampaging through the world forcing life into women as fast as I was draining life out of them. I couldn't understand him. He was a mystery. After the chief of police had finished describing the arrest, the Leopard's father had a few words to say about it. The boy was popular at school, worked for the church and loved his mother. The father couldn't understand what had happened to his son.

When the news was finished there was a beauty contest. I think it was called Miss Heavenly Body. There was a line of chunky girls in swimsuits and bleached hair, grinning like loonies and puffing out their breasts whenever they caught the judges' eye. The presenter asked each of them in turn what she would do if she won the title, Miss Heavenly Body. One said she would work in a refuge for mentally handicapped animals. Another said she would open a beauty parlour so that every woman could learn to be so beautiful. The girl who won the title promised to work for peace and a greater understanding between the nations of the world. Everyone whistled and cheered. She might have been the pope. They pinned a cardboard crown to her head and she burst into tears.

I thought, it's a shame that the Leopard didn't see Miss Heavenly Body. He might have enjoyed it. But it was not until I had crawled into bed that I remembered my conversation with Frank and understood suddenly what had driven the Leopard to a life of plunder and rape. He had become a victim of his own addiction. He continued to play the part of the Leopard because, once he had tasted the forbidden fruit, he could not resist. And if such a fate could fall upon a mild young man who worked for the church and loved his mother, what were my own chances of survival?

*

A few days before Christmas, Dorothy rang me and demanded that I spend the holiday at the butcher's table.

"It's a very generous invitation," I said "But I think I'd feel like an orphan saved from the snow."

I heard Dorothy cluck in exasperation, "You'll feel even more of an orphan if you spend Christmas alone in your miserable little room," she said.

"But I'm not prepared," I said "I haven't even thought about the holiday . . ."

"There's nothing to think about, Mackerel. Just stick a toothbrush in your pocket and come down."

"I'd love to see you again," I said.

"There's something I want to give you . . ." she said in a whisper.

I didn't argue. There wasn't time. I swept along Bond Street and into Piccadilly in a frenzy of Christmas shopping. I bought a box of sugared plums, a potted Stilton and a crusty bottle of vintage port, a photograph album in ginger leather, a silver brooch and a box of Japanese indoor fireworks that proved to be damp and disappointing.

I packed my gifts in black tissue paper and silver ribbon, loaded the Volkswagen and, early one morning, began the long ride west to the Atlantic. Dorothy had given me detailed instructions of the route; the roads to take and the towns to avoid, and I arrived on their doorstep a little before noon.

They lived in a splendid Victorian house surrounded by gravel and rhododendrons. It had five bedrooms, three marble bathrooms and stained glass in the attic windows. Dorothy had decorated the rooms with holly and mistletoe and laid a log fire in every grate. But the heart of the house was the kitchen and as soon as I arrived Dorothy led me by the hand into its welcome heat.

"You look pale," she said happily as she surveyed me, "You don't eat enough.

"I left before breakfast."

"I've got some ham. Throw your coat in one of those chairs and we'll have breakfast together."

"No, please don't bother," I said, "I never eat breakfast."

Dorothy looked flustered. "Never mind. We'll call it lunch."

I took off my coat and sat down to watch Dorothy dash about the kitchen, burning toast and spilling coffee. The kitchen ran the entire length of the building and in the summer was a breeding ground for cats. It smelt like a restaurant, looked like a nursery and sounded like the engine room of a big yacht. A solid pine table with scrubbed wooden chairs stood in the centre of the room. The walls were loaded with shelves of bowls and bottles, books and toys, novelty biscuit tins and teapots shaped like cottages; while all around the constant throbbing of machines in shadow; dishwashers, refrigerators, mincers, grinders, shredders and blenders. There were so many machines that even Dorothy could not explain them all.

A huge, snow white Kelvinator stood in the far corner of the room. It was the size of a sofa and when you stood beside it you could feel the floor vibrate beneath your feet. Inside this gleaming monolith lay the carcasses of sheep and pigs, trimmed, gutted and beautiful with frost. I don't believe Dorothy ever used it because she would accept nothing but fresh red meat. It was Archie's own, private freezer and he used it as a small museum in which to store his favourite corpses.

There had been no sign of Archie when I arrived and after we had gorged on ham and pickles and very black toast I asked Dorothy about him.

"Oh, he's not here."

"Is everything all right?" I ventured.

"How do you mean?"

"Well, you haven't been fighting . . .?"

"Don't be silly. He's as tender as a lamb. We never fight."

"Oh."

"Archie is working. He's up to his armpits in turkey entrails."

"Yes, of course, I was forgetting."

"You won't see very much of him until Christmas Day – and

he probably won't recognise you until the day after Boxing Day – he usually goes to sleep for Christmas."

I glanced up from my coffee cup and caught Dorothy staring at me. I smiled. She continued to stare without expression. I stopped smiling. She licked the corner of her mouth and caught a crumb with a flick of her tongue. And then I blushed until my scalp prickled and my collar felt damp against my neck. I knew she was thinking about the game and, at the same time, I knew she would deny everything if I dared remind her of it. There was silence. It was as if we had made a guest appearance in each other's dream and to have discussed the dream would have broken the spell. But the silence told me that my nights under the butcher's roof might be long and turbulent.

"I'll show you to your room," she said.

I gathered my luggage and followed her slowly up the stairs. Her ankles seemed to sprout, white and surprised, from an old pair of cotton trousers. Her hair was longer than I remembered and flopped into her eyes whenever she bent her head so that she would rake it back impatiently with a comb of fingers.

I loved her lean greyhound face and narrow shoulders. I loved her with a marvellous surrender. I might have dragged her down upon the stairs and torn the buttons from her trousers, I might have forced her against the wall and opened her shirt, but I had surrendered long ago to the rules of Dorothy's secret game and could only wait, nervously, for her instructions.

We spent the rest of that first day together talking and laughing, drinking and playing cards. Archie came home around midnight and, after crushing my hand briefly between his own great fists, sank mournfully into an armchair and closed his eyes. He looked old and gaunt. His face was grey with fatigue. But a hot whisky seemed to revive him and he was soon strong enough to open his eyes again and smile. I asked him about the price of Christmas turkey and his smile broadened into a grin. He asked me if I had found an occupation for myself and I told him about my history of conjuring. It required a great deal of research, I explained, and would probably take several years to complete. I had discussed the book at such length with Frank that I had started to believe in it.

Archie sat and nodded his head in approval. He was always concerned with how I managed to pass the time because he felt that a man without regular employment was in perpetual danger of becoming a criminal or going mad with boredom and booze. His own success as a butcher – he owned most of the butchers' shops in three counties – had done nothing to diminish his own appetite for simple, hard labour. Where another man in the same position might have sat behind a desk and sucked a cigar, Archie spent his time on the sawdust floor, dressed in a bloody apron.

Archie sat and nodded, but his head was heavy and his chin fell against his chest. He began to snore. I helped Dorothy haul him upstairs and said goodnight. I went to bed and lay awake for hours, listening for the slightest movement in the darkness. But nothing disturbed the silence. I fell asleep and was not woken until late the following morning when Dorothy brought me coffee.

"Wake up, Mackerel," she shouted as she dragged at the curtains. "It's late."

"What's happening?" I roared thickly from under my pillow.

"We're going shopping – come on – get dressed."

When I opened my eyes I saw that she was already dressed and her face was painted. I crawled from the warm sheets, stood up and staggered across the carpet. Dorothy pushed the coffee into my hands and left me to search for my clothes. The room was full of narcotic perfume.

It was the day before Christmas Eve, a brilliant, cold day with frost on the lawns. We drove into town and stopped at one of the big department stores. I don't remember the name of the store but it thought itself important enough to carry a restaurant and Father Christmas in Wonderland. Dorothy swept through the crowds, weaving from counter to counter, dragging me behind her like a sulking child. She was wrapped in a thick ball of fur and she snarled like a racoon whenever she was jostled or pushed.

"Look, do you like them?" she demanded as she pulled a string of beads from a counter display. They were crude glass beads the colours of cheap soap.

"Yes, they're pretty," I said without conviction.

Dorothy thrust the beads into the pocket of her coat.

"What are you doing?" I gasped in her ear. I couldn't believe what had happened.

"I'm stealing them," she said as we pushed our way through the crowd.

"But you can't do that – they'll catch you," I muttered fiercely under my breath.

"They never catch me – they're too slow. Come on," she whispered and led me away.

"How long have you been doing it?" I whispered. I was shocked.

"Oh, years and years. It's a hobby. I'll show you how to do it if you're interested, Mackerel."

"But it's against the law," I squeaked.

"Yes, I know," said Dorothy.

"But what would happen if Archie found out about it?" I demanded.

"Oh, I expect he'd cut my hands off," she said with a grin.

"But . . ."

"Shut up and stuff this in your pocket," she murmured. Her hand was searching for the pockets of my overcoat. I caught her hand and she pressed a bracelet into my palm. I pushed my hands into my pockets and kept them there. The bracelet burned the lining of my coat like a baked potato. I just couldn't believe what was happening. I was convinced we were being watched. When I looked around I thought I saw a detective in every face in the crowd. It was terrible.

We roamed through the store, stuffing our pockets with whatever trinket caught Dorothy's evil eye. I cannot understand why she played the thief. It was crazy. Perhaps she did it for the excitement, the sheer hell of practising her sleight of hand in the full glare of the counter girls. It's possible. It certainly scared the hell out of me. By the time Dorothy had grown tired of her sins my shirt was soaked with sweat and my ears were ringing.

I wanted to sneak away through the back of the store and make my escape. But Dorothy had not finished. She laughed when I pleaded to be taken home and insisted that we rest our feet in the restaurant where she ordered coffee and cake. The chocolate sponge felt like sawdust in my mouth.

"This is terrible," I hissed, glancing around for detectives dressed as waitresses.

"It's harmless," she shrugged.

"No," I glared, "It's very silly and very dangerous."

She sucked at the edge of her coffee cup. "I don't take any risks," she murmured.

"Yes, but if they catch you . . ."

"If they didn't try to catch you it wouldn't be exciting," she explained.

The next day we bought a pine tree, dragged it into the kitchen and planted its stump in a barrel. It filled the room with a mysterious green light. It was so tall that the delicate scented tip was pressed against the ceiling.

Dorothy dressed the tree with everything we had stolen. It was a strange assortment; a set of screwdrivers, a bracelet, a string of beads, a lipstick, a chocolate rabbit, a packet of false fingernails, a card of darning thread and a box of crayons. Those treasures hung from the great tree like gifts selected for a tea party in a lunatic asylum. It was a very curious display.

We did not visit my mother for Christmas. I phoned the hospital and a doctor told me the old lady was depressed and under sedation. She had not asked about me and he was hoping she would sleep for a fortnight. He wanted her to rest her brains. Dorothy's parents, the grocers, were still alive and in rude health but they had refused to speak to Dorothy since she had entered the butcher's bed and she had not seen them since her wedding. Archie must have owned parents, I suppose, but he never spoke of them. We were three Christmas orphans and we were content.

Christmas dinner was a roast goose stuffed with apples soaked in rum. Dorothy took great care to dress for the occasion. She wore a black and white pinstriped jacket and a narrow black skirt with a bouncing pleat. Beneath the jacket she wore a white cotton shirt and a small bow-tie. She looked mischievous and wonderfully wicked. Whenever she threw back her head to laugh, tiny blue diamonds flashed in her ears.

After dinner I presented Archie with the photograph album and Dorothy with the silver brooch – a tiny pair of polished handcuffs. They seemed very pleased with these little offerings and spent a long time thanking me for my kindness while I pretended they were mere trifles and did not deserve such admiration. Then Archie presented me with a magnificent set of butcher's knives in a polished walnut box. He tried to shrug off my thanks but nothing could hide the pleasure in his face as he stared at the box. They were beautiful weapons, blue as mirrors and cold, cold against the skin. I saw, at once, that they were not humble kitchen knives made for slicing sausage or splitting fowl. They were heavy, ceremonial blades to be hoarded and treasured for their beauty.

When all the fluster and flattery was finished we sat for a while to drink the bottle of port. Archie began to dream of Christmas past.

"In the old days, I mean the Middle Ages, it was a good time to be a butcher," he said wistfully.

"I thought the people starved," I said.

"Ah, yes, *some* of the people starved. But not nearly so many as starve today. I mean, there were fewer people in the world. There were fewer mouths to try and feed," he explained.

"It was a struggle to survive," argued Dorothy.

But Archie wasn't listening to our doubts about the quality of life in the Middle Ages. He was dreaming again of meat.

"They used to fatten up a swan – they ate swans in those days – and then they would stuff it with a goose. They'd stuff the goose with a duck and the duck with a chicken and the chicken with something else. Each time the bird got smaller and smaller until they'd finish the very centre of the thing with a little budgerigar."

"They didn't eat budgerigars in the Middle Ages," protested Dorothy.

Archie gave her a long, old-fashioned look. "Well, whatever

it was they used, it was damned small and the butchers must have been damned fat," he said.

We talked and sipped at the port for an hour or more before Archie began to grow uncomfortable, yawn extravagantly and knead his eyes with his knuckles. Finally, mumbling his apologies, he staggered to his feet and shuffled away to bed. He looked happy, exhausted and very drunk.

Dorothy was left to entertain me. She filled my glass with port and smiled.

"They're very beautiful knives," I said.

"He likes you," she said carelessly, as if she were discussing a dog.

She led me from the kitchen and through into a smaller room at the back of the house. It was filled by an ancient sofa and a huge display of potted plants. Tiles on the floor and the walls of raw brick. It was hot and aromatic and dark.

The only light came from the embers of a small log fire that cracked and fizzed in the hearth. She sat beside me in the lap of the sofa and stared up at my face.

"He looked tired . . ." I ventured.

"He *is* tired . . ." she said with confidence. "He's so tired he'll probably sleep until this time tomorrow."

"You spiked his port," I whispered.

Dorothy smiled again. "While he's asleep I can give you my Christmas present," she said.

She threw back her head and unclipped the little bow-tie at her throat. She flipped off her jacket and stood up to unfasten her skirt. I sat and watched her undress in silence. Her fingers picked at the buttons of her shirt. A log flared in the hearth and her fingernails flashed like flakes of glass. She was wearing white silk stockings. Her legs were so long that the stockings barely seemed to reach above her knees. She peeled the stockings off and used them to tie my hands behind my back.

"Are you comfortable?" she said.

"Yes," I said. The knots were so tight I thought the silk would cut my wrists.

When she was satisfied that I was harmless she guided me from the sofa and made me kneel down on the floor. Then she picked up my port, stood before me and let the thick crimson wine trickle down her belly and worm its way between her legs. I was amazed. My mouth dropped open and my tongue fell out. I began to drink.

London seemed unlovely and forlorn when I returned. The crowds in Victoria Station were bleary-eyed somnambulists, dragging themselves into the city, wretched and silent. But God had not been slumbering. During the twelve days of Christmas an earthquake in Italy had destroyed seven villages and killed fifteen people, an Air France 747 had burst into flames over Chicago and dropped 280 people from a great height, a family had drowned in a Greek flood and an avalanche had buried an hotel in the Alps. These were all described as Acts of God and the police were not prepared to detain anyone for questioning.

I sat at home through the worst of the January weather and dreamt of my sport. Whenever the storms lifted I went shopping for knives. I favoured street markets and charity shops, hunting for old kitchen knives that could not be traced back to some fancy department store. I bought a small whetstone and amused myself by sharpening the blades and trimming the dull shapes into narrow spikes.

It was such an absorbing occupation that I quickly acquired a large collection. But I resisted the temptation of carrying a favourite blade in my pocket when I went walking in the streets. I was determined to deny myself the pleasures of the kill for as long as I could possibly endure it. Frank's observation that the Soho murderer was an addict still worried me and I wanted to test the extent of my addiction. It wasn't easy. Several times I packed a bag with my Polaroid and rubber gloves, but each time refused to surrender to the excitement and drugged myself by watching television until I fell asleep.

It was Frank's birthday in the first week of February and we went out to supper with two of his lady friends. They were called, I remember, Thumper and Frosty and were waiting for us when we arrived at the restaurant. I usually avoid eating in restaurants and I did not relish the prospect of meeting Frank's friends, but it was a special occasion so I wore my best suit and my widest smile.

The one called Frosty had hair the colour of pulpit brass, cropped very short to expose her ears. She had a pudding face and a small but very lugubrious mouth. She seemed to be on the most intimate terms with the birthday boy who kept patting her rump and chuckling to himself.

The one called Thumper was a tall, pale woman with dark hair that had been lacquered into stiff ringlets. She had a long, narrow face cut like a tribal mask, the nose straight and the eyes slanted. The eyes were painted with little blue rainbows. She was wearing a strawberry satin skirt and a black blazer. Beneath the blazer she seemed to be wearing nothing at all except a long gold thread that hung from her neck. She sat next to me and when I asked her why she was called Thumper, she laughed and told me not to be so impatient. Her laugh was like a fire alarm and made me blush.

It was a huge, sprawling restaurant with a dance floor and orchestra. But Frank directed us to the shelter of a corner table and, when we were settled, asked his friends what they wanted to drink.

"Champagne," said Frosty without hesitation.

Frank only laughed and ordered red wine. Thumper gulped down a glass of the stuff as soon as it was poured and then asked me how I earned my living. I tried to explain about the book I was writing, the history of conjuring and the lives of the great magicians. I hesitated a few times because I knew Frank was listening and he knew as much about the book as I did and would notice if there were any obvious mistakes in my account. Sod it, I thought as I blushed and mumbled my way through the deceit, I'll start writing this damned book tomorrow instead of just talking about it. But before I had finished talking I saw Thumper smirking at me.

"What's wrong?" I said, blushing again.

"Do you have one of those little magic wands?" she said.

I frowned, I didn't understand.

"He can do tricks with it," spluttered Frosty and the two women roared with laughter.

"You shouldn't laugh," sniggered Thumper, "He's a conjurer and you never know what he's got up his sleeve."

"I'm not interested in his sleeves," wheezed Frosty, "Show me what he's got down his pants."

"Stop teasing him," said Frank. Frosty winked at me and filled my glass. Beneath the table I felt Thumper squeeze my knee. I tried to ignore them. But they would not stop their silly whispering or translating my most innocent remarks into their own filthy language.

I was afraid it might spoil Frank's evening but to my surprise he became quite drunk and could barely fit three words together. He didn't touch his food but chain-smoked and chuckled and ran his hand under Frosty's dress.

It was hard work trying to keep Thumper engaged in any sensible conversation. She began to press herself too close against me and leered at my blushes. I was explaining the principles of levitation when she suddenly cupped my chin in her hand and squeezed until my mouth popped open between her fingers. Then she slid a finger inside, running it along the edge of my teeth. While she examined my mouth she stared at me with her strange, slanted eyes.

"It's time to go home," she said.

I glanced helplessly across at Frosty and Frank. They were so drunk they couldn't see across the room and it took them several attempts to stand up and stagger free from the table. It was a nightmare. I don't know how we struggled home but, somehow, we managed it.

Once I had dragged Frank into the safety of his apartment I was anxious to say goodnight and escape. But Frank seemed to recover his senses, produced a bottle of Scotch and demanded that I stay for a final birthday drink. The fumes as he pulled the cork were enough to knock me out but Frank threw back his head and took a swig. The Scotch splashed his chin and he tried to wipe it with his sleeve. Then Frosty made a grab for the bottle but she was too drunk to hold it against her mouth and fell down in a heap, nursing the bottle in her arms.

"Perhaps we should put her to bed," I suggested to Thumper but she only sniggered and said something foolish.

While we watched, Frosty grunted and began to crawl towards the bedroom on her hands and knees. Frank saw her disappear through the door and, with some difficulty, managed to follow her into the dark.

I wanted to leave but Thumper took hold of my arm and dragged me off in pursuit of them. She was very strong. Her fingernails punctured my wrist.

We found Frosty and Frank sprawled together on the floor beside the bed. Frosty had managed to remove one of Frank's shoes but could not find the strength to throw it away. She sat nursing it in her arms and grinned blindly at the ceiling. The birthday boy had torn open the buttons of his trousers but had pulled out nothing more deadly than a thick twist of his shirt. He tweaked the shirt in his fingers and looked puzzled, as if he suspected it did not belong to him. When he saw us approach he promptly buried his head beneath Frosty's skirts. They giggled and wriggled together for a few moments and then Frosty fainted. Frank began to snore.

I turned to leave but Thumper clung tighter to my wrist and pulled me back into the room.

"Where are you going?" she whispered.

"I have to go home."

"What's your problem?" she demanded impatiently. "Don't you like women?"

"Yes, I like women," I said, "My mother was a woman. But I would prefer not to – you know – get involved with you."

"You don't have to fucking marry me."

"I'd rather go home, thank you."

"Well, it's Frank's money," she yawned, "I don't care if you don't have the balls for it. I'm tired. I could use the sleep."

"You don't understand," I said.

"What's the mystery?" she shrugged.

"I have some very unusual tastes," I said darkly. It was a hollow boast but I was trying to cool her ardour and make her release me.

"Would you like me to fetch you a choir boy?" she sneered.

I was wounded by her insults. My ears were burning. I could have snapped her silly neck across my knee. I wanted to tell her about the risks she was taking in taunting such a dangerous killer. I wanted to shake off my disguise and frighten her with the face of death.

"You might regret those words," I threatened.

"Yeah," she sneered, "And you might shit a string of pearls."

"Shut your mouth," I gasped, "You're disgusting."

"Go home and play with yourself," she said and stumbled back to her friend beside the bed. She poked about under Frosty's skirts for a few moments and recovered Frank's head which she cradled gently in her lap, stroking the hair from his eyes and pulling at the buttons of his shirt. I could have throttled her with my bare hands. But I turned instead and left the room. It had not been a great success.

For the next two weeks I stayed at home, sulking and planning my grand history of conjuring. I wasn't going to be teased again. I had no doubt that I *could* write such a book and the more I thought about it, the more excited I became about the idea. I had already collected all the important reference books on the subject – including a rare copy of Hubert's Conjuring Encyclopedia – and assembled quite a valuable collection of old theatre programmes. So I sharpened my pencils and started to scribble and dream of my masterpiece. The weather was foul and I was happy to be sitting at home beside the fire.

Everything was fine until I cracked a tooth. It was a big molar and it seemed to explode in the middle of a bacon sandwich, leaving me with a mouthful of bread and shrapnel. I swallowed a lot of it but rescued some of the sharper fragments. I put them in an envelope for safety because I thought a dentist might want to see them. It didn't give me any pain but the stump looked dreadful and I knew it would need some attention. Frank, who still couldn't remember anything about his birthday, gave me the name and address of his dentist and insisted that I make an appointment the same day.

His name was Israel Casper and he worked in Belgravia, restoring the shine on the smiles of the rich, or repairing them, tastefully, in porcelain and gold. The waiting room contained six armchairs gathered around a flower arrangement on an antique table. I sat there for ten minutes, sweating and pretending to read *Country Life*, before I was led blindly to the chair. Casper was as big as a walrus and nearly as bad-tempered. He gestured towards the chair. I sat down and he adjusted the machine, unfolding me until I was staring helplessly at the cracks in the ceiling.

"What's the trouble?" he demanded.

"I've broken a tooth," I said. "I've brought along the bits and pieces – you know – in case you want them." I offered him the envelope containing the precious relics.

He snorted and took hold of the packet with a finger and thumb, as if he were handling a turd, and cast it aside.

"Throw it away, nurse," he muttered.

He tried to force all his fingers into my mouth at the same time, as if he were measuring something. When he was finished he washed his hands.

"Will you take out the stump?" I asked gingerly. I wanted to know about anaesthetics. I appreciate a good anaesthetic when I visit a dentist.

"Good God, no, we'll use the stump as the foundation for a new tooth," he said. "I don't believe in extractions." He made Extractions sound like a lewd branch of the Quakers. "Your mouth is horrible," he added as he dried his hands in a paper towel.

Then the telephone rang. He snatched it up, snorted, swore and dropped it again with a clatter.

"I'm sorry, I have to go out for a few minutes," he announced, "Keep him amused, Jane."

It was not until he called the nurse by name that I noticed she was in the room. But when I tilted my head against my shoulder and swivelled my eyes I could see her legs and her white canvas shoes.

"Would you like to sit up for a few minutes?" she asked me as soon as the walrus had left us alone.

"Thanks," I said, struggling to regain my balance and

knocking my head against the lamp.

"Did you hurt yourself?"

"No," I gasped through my tears.

"Would you like a glass of water?" she asked as I rubbed my head. She was no more than twenty years old and as delicate as a pixie. Was it the sight of the buttons on her white nylon coat to remind me of the voluptuous Figg or was it simply the warmth of her face as she smiled at me that ignited my desire? I don't know. I stared at her as if she were the first woman I had ever seen. I could not stop myself.

While I drank the water she moved about the room, arranging instruments in a metal tray, and my eyes followed her everywhere. She asked me if I had been treated by the walrus in the past and I said that I hadn't, although he had been highly recommended to me. She asked me if I worked in an office and I said, no, I was studying magic and then, for fear that she might misunderstand me, I explained about the book. She didn't snigger or ask me if I played with my wand. It was a good moment. She asked me if I ever went to see foreign films and, in an effort to please her and keep her talking, I nodded and smiled. Her face was small and full of freckles. She wore her hair short but it was growing wild and as curly as brambles, falling over her ears and into her eyes. She kept sweeping it back from her face as she talked. She was chattering like a little bird about some old Japanese character who made samurai movies and she said that the film was showing in Oxford Street at the Academy but she hadn't managed to go and see it although it was already in its last week.

"Perhaps we could go and see it together?" I suggested and blushed at the sound of my own voice. I had caught myself thinking aloud! I sat, flushed and tense in the sudden silence, and tried hopelessly to find more words so that I could cover my mistake and manoeuvre the conversation into neutral territory. I felt ridiculous. I was already in enough trouble without Nurse Jane trotting out and complaining that I was making a nuisance of myself. But asking the question had rendered me speechless and I could only sit there with my mouth open.

"Yes," she said, "I'd like that."

The answer was almost as alarming as the question and I continued to sit speechless and peer anxiously at my shoes while Jane smiled and quietly polished a metal probe.

"Tonight?" I finally managed to croak.

"Tonight would be nice, but tomorrow would be better," she said after a moment's thought.

"Where shall we meet?"

"I'll meet you at the box office at seven thirty," she said and smiled again.

I don't remember what happened to me in the following ten minutes. The walrus came back and poked around in my mouth, made my gums bleed and told me to make another appointment. I went home and practised smiling in the mirror.

Was it so simple? Can a love affair begin with a smile, a gesture, a few polite words? Nothing more had happened and yet I felt transformed, exhilarated by the experience. I had taken a broken tooth to the dentist and gone home with my heart bubbling and my eyes cloudy with happiness. If the memory of my ordeal at the hands of Frosty and Thumper had not still rankled in me I am sure I would never have found the courage to approach Nurse Jane. So perhaps Frank's birthday really had been something to celebrate.

We met at the Academy box office, as arranged, and although she would not allow me to buy her ticket, she let me buy a bag of peppermints instead. She was wearing a white cotton dress and a pair of red shoes. The dress was printed with tiny bunches of red flowers. I noticed, for the first time, that her eyes were brown. A dark, river brown, speckled with brighter spots of rust. She wore no make-up, except perhaps for a little mascara so that the freckles shone through and made her look like a country girl.

As we walked to our seats she turned to smile, exposing her teeth, and I saw that some of the teeth were crooked, one overlapping the other in a friendly jumble. It was an observation that made me absurdly happy. She wasn't beautiful. Men were never moved to whistle at her in the street or leer at her across restaurant tables. But there were moments, when she threw back her head to laugh or wrinkled her nose in concentration, when she seemed to me almost painfully beautiful and it made me love her more because her beauty was something she shared with the Mackerel alone and did not parade in the street.

She sat silently in the dark, staring up at the screen while I sucked peppermints beside her and wondered what she was thinking about. The film was a load of nonsense about fat men in heavy armour shouting at each other in dusty courtyards. It wasn't too bad. When it was finished we had a hamburger and I drove her home.

She lived in two rooms in a house in Chelsea. She had a mother in Portsmouth and a brother, I think, who worked in Paris. She had only been working in London for eighteen months and most of that time had been spent with the walrus. We sat together in the car, talking, and she said she would like to see me again.

"Perhaps we could go and see another film?" I suggested boldly and wished, at once, that I had more imagination.

"Yes," she said, as if it were a most original notion, "That would be fun. Do you have a favourite?"

"Well . . . that's difficult," I said doubtfully. "There are so many films to choose . . ."

"The Charlie Chaplin season starts next month," she said, "Do you like Charlie Chaplin?"

Do I *like* him? For you, Nurse Jane, I'll laugh like a hyena, cackle so I burst a vein, hoot until I'm sick. "Yes," I said.

"Good," she said, "It's a date."

"How shall I find you again?"

"Oh, phone the surgery. The receptionist will always take a message."

We said goodnight and she kissed the corner of my mouth. And that was how it began. It was not until the next day that I discovered Charlie Chaplin would not arrive in town for another three weeks.

During March, to keep myself amused, I performed the Hammersmith Housewife Murders. I carried my equipment in a little suitcase and planned to walk from door to door like a brush salesman. It was a Monday morning and no one had the time or the curiosity to offer me a glance as I worked my way along the street.

In the first house I found a fat woman chopping carrots in a narrow kitchen full of steam and jangling music. Her hair was white and her eyes were red, as if she had lived in the steam for years and years and slowly cooked herself like a big, boiled codfish. I offered her some nonsense about the drains and demanded to look at her pipes.

"Pipes? There's nothing wrong with my pipes," she said cheerfully. "It's my tubes that give me the trouble," She tapped her chest with her fingers and gave a fruity cough. She seemed to think it was very comical.

"There have been complaints," I said.

"Complaints?" she said sharply. "Who complained?"

"I couldn't tell you," I said with a shrug of the shoulders. "The office handles all the paperwork."

"So what are you going to do about it?" she asked.

"The drains are too shallow, that's the problem," I explained. "Will you check the waste pipe under the sink?"

I pulled on my rubber gloves and watched her crawl on her hands and knees into the cupboard beneath the sink. She was wearing a blue cotton housecoat and a pair of threadbare slippers. I knelt down beside her and waited for her to emerge from the gloom. She smelt of soap and onions.

"Which one is the waste pipe?" she called out in exasperation. "There are lots of pipes down here and they're scrambled together."

"The waste pipe is the one shaped like a horseshoe," I called out as I took up the carrot knife.

"I can't find it," she grumbled. "They're all different shapes and sizes. This one feels a funny shape but I don't think . . ."

When she sensed that I was not following her guided tour of the plumbing she began to crawl backwards into the daylight. She was still on her knees when I kissed her ear and probed her brains with the knife. She groaned and fell sideways onto the floor. The blood began to percolate gently through her scalp and stained her hair. I watched the untidy white curls blush at their roots and darken until her hair had turned a warm and beautiful shade of geranium. It was a remarkable transformation. She looked like a young woman again.

I tidied her up, opened her coat and closed her eyes. She was wearing a heavy corset spun from pink rubber cobwebs and elastic bandage, held together by steel rivets. She made a lovely picture.

I despatched three housewives in the same morning, rang their doorbells and charmed my way into their hearts. I told them I had been instructed to inspect their drains and they seemed happy enough with my excuses. I fled home exhausted and on the edge of collapse. I took a bath and ate a small lunch. I pinned my Polaroids to the frame of the bedroom mirror and then went to bed. I had taken such risks that morning – anything might have gone wrong! I might have been disturbed by neighbours. I might have walked into a Tupperware party. It was a wild madness to offer murder door-to-door in broad daylight. Yet I had never been so excited or so terrified, I had never before known such exhilaration from the knives.

The murders were reported on the late news the same day and Hammersmith became a fortress for the rest of the year. Women carried whistles and pepper-pots in their handbags. Men mounted patrols in the streets at night. But I never went to Hammersmith again.

If I am caught I'll tell them that God made me use the blades. I can't confess that I killed purely for pleasure. They wouldn't believe me. They couldn't understand. I'll tell them that I felt it was my duty by God. That's what they will tell the soldiers before they are driven away and fed into the mouths of the nuclear cannon. I know they would prefer to think of me as a madman. So I shall tell them that God phoned me and gave me instructions. They'll breathe a sigh of relief and say, this poor man is a victim of some violent madness, take him away and wash out his brains. They'll offer me a hospital bed instead of a prison cell. It happens. It works. They'll tap my head and measure my skull, watch me through the keyhole for five or ten years and finally turn me out on the street. I know it's crazy but I have to tell them what they want to believe.

The weather improved. The cold and blustering rains retreated beneath the glare of a brilliant sun. The crowds in Victoria Station were flecked with splashes of summer colour, the men wore their jackets over their arms and the women walked briskly, exposing pale legs under cotton skirts.

Charlie Chaplin came to town and I took Jane to see him twice, driving her safely to her door in Chelsea at the end of each evening. We exchanged phone numbers and began calling each other at odd times, talking about nothing in particular. I found myself collecting snippets of gossip and using them as excuses to call and talk. When I went walking I caught myself searching for her in the streets, although I knew she would be busy at work with the walrus. And then, on the first hot Saturday in April, I packed the car with a picnic and drove Nurse Jane into the country.

We drove for about an hour, until the industrial sprawl ran into suburbs and the suburbs ran into open fields, woodland and sky. As we left the city behind, Nurse Jane began to grow happier, whistling like a schoolboy and feeding me slices of apple which she cut with a penknife.

"I hate the city," she said cheerfully.

"It's not so bad," I said, "We could have had our picnic in Hyde Park."

"And share it with thousands of other people," she scoffed.

I turned off the road and we bounced some distance up an old cart track to the brow of a thickly wooded hill. When I switched off the engine there was nothing to be heard but the sound of the wind in the trees. The branches formed a vaulted ceiling of green and sepia shadow. The earth was black beneath our feet. We left the car and carried the picnic into the sunlight. We opened a bottle of wine and attacked a great turkey pie with the knife.

When we were finished we sprawled on the ground and stared at the sky. Jane was wearing an old shirt and a baggy pair of corduroy trousers which were gathered and tied by a leather belt. As she felt the sun begin to warm her face she conducted an elaborate undressing. She rolled her shirt sleeves, unbuttoned her collar, unbuckled the belt and pulled her trouser-legs over her knees. She kicked off her shoes and wriggled her toes in the long grass. Finally she threw back her head, narrowed her eyes and invited the sun to paint her freckles.

"When I was a little girl," she said presently, "there was a pond at the back of the house – in an old meadow – and we used to go down there after school and lie on our stomachs and peer into the water and look for fish. We used to believe that a monster pike lived in the pond and we dared each other to trail our fingers among the weeds . . ."

"Did you ever see it?"

"No, but sometimes a boy called Harris would jump from the bushes with his willy hanging out and that would make us scream."

"What happened to him?"

"He grew up," she said with a shrug.

"That's a pity."

"And then there was a secret place we called the Witch Stone where the blackberries grew as fat as plums and we'd gorge ourselves on them until our fingers and faces were stained red and blue."

"Weren't you sick?"

"All the time," she said, "The blackberries were full of worms."

A crow tumbled in the sky above our heads.

"Don't you miss it?" I said.

"What?"

"Everything . . the pike . . . the pond."

"Oh, that's all gone. They filled in the pond and built houses on the meadow. Everything's gone." Her hair fell into her eyes and she scooped it back with her hand.

"And the Witch Stone?"

"Oh yes, the Witch Stone is still there – but now they call it the Happy Hamburger."

She made the past seem like a threadbare carpet which was being rolled up behind her, as she used it, day by day. Every stick or stone in her childhood seemed to have been destroyed as soon as she had touched it. Perhaps that's why she was so interested in the preservation of teeth.

Later, when the wine had muddled our heads and carried us to the edges of sleep I spoke about the sea and my mother's hotel. I told her that on winters' nights there were violent storms that flung fish against the hotel windows and in the mornings I was made to collect them and fry them for breakfast. But she would not believe me. I confessed that my secret name was Mackerel but she only wrinkled her nose and looked doubtful.

"Why did they call you Mackerel?"

"Because my eyes were so big and my mouth was always open."

"They're lovely eyes," she said.

Beneath our feet the hill rolled away into small fields marked by hedges, beyond the fields a blue smudge of forest against the sky. A tractor knitted its way across one corner of a field, followed closely by a squadron of gulls.

"Are you happy?" I asked.

"Yes, I'm happy," she said in surprise. "Why do you ask?"

"Oh, I don't know – it's important – I want you to be happy," I said, hoping to disguise my blush beneath a frown.

"You're such a lovely, gentle person," she said. She took my hand and kissed the fingers, one by one. "Sweet William."

I wanted to gather her into my arms and cradle her against me, I wanted to stretch forward and smother her mouth with kisses. But I did nothing. I chewed my lip and counted her freckles.

I killed only once during April and May. It was a warm, acid-blue Sunday morning and Nurse Jane was in Portsmouth to visit her mother. I had been exploring the streets around Earl's Court and was strolling back towards the VW when a figure lurched from a shop doorway and clutched at my arm.

It was such an unexpected assault that I almost shouted in alarm and fled. I was carrying my equipment in a little leather shopping bag and I could not afford to run any risks in the street. But when I turned to confront my assailant I discovered that I was being mauled by nothing more fearsome than a big Australian girl in a damp and crumpled party frock. She was very drunk and looked as if she had spent the night sheltering in a doorway. She was shivering and her hair was tangled.

"Good morning," I said.

The girl peered at me for some moments and then took her fingers out of my arm.

"Can I help you?" I asked.

"Yeah, you can take me home," she mumbled in a queasy voice, "I don't feel strong enough to walk it alone."

"It's a pleasure," I said.

"Thanks."

"Where do you live?"

"Nevern Square – it's just around the corner," she said, nodding her head in the general direction.

"It's a beautiful morning," I suggested.

"It was a terrible party," she croaked.

We searched around in the doorway for her handbag and then I escorted her slowly into Nevern Square. It took several minutes because she hobbled like an old woman and moaned and wiped her face and generally complained. She finally staggered up the steps of a dirty apartment block and wrenched the key from her handbag. I helped her open the heavy front door and she invited me into her room.

"I don't want to trouble you," I said.

"It's no trouble," she said, "And you deserve a beer for helping me."

I accepted with a smile, moving with dainty steps, careful not to smudge the furniture with a careless fingerprint. As soon as she had entered the safety of her room she seemed to recover her strength. She brushed her hair with her hand and yawned.

"Jesus, I'm hungry," she announced. "Will you have a sandwich?"

"Thank you," I said, "I'd like that."

She gave me a beer and began to search through a cupboard for bread. She told me she was Marlene from New South Wales and worked as a receptionist in Piccadilly. I sat and watched her in silence while she stood at a little table and hacked at the loaf with a long knife.

It was an exquisite moment. It was the moment when I knew I had again been offered the power of life and death. I could sit in the chair with the Sunday sunlight warm on the dusty carpet and wait for my sandwich. I could sip at the beer and watch her legs move beneath the stained party frock. I could eat the sandwich, brush the crumbs from my lap, stand up and leave the room. I could stroll back to the VW and drive home. Or I could pull on my faithful rubber gloves so neatly concealed in the shopping bag at my feet, stand up and slip my hand around the broad satin waist, taking her wrist with my other hand, guiding the knife against her neck. I could press myself against her rump and pull the blade towards me.

"What will you have in your sandwich?" she said as she bent down and pushed her face in the fridge. "I've got cheese, corned beef, sardines and apricots."

"Apricots?"

"Yeah, tinned apricots. They taste great in a sandwich." She kicked shut the fridge door and returned to the table with a dozen wrinkled apricots floating in a bowl of syrup. She fished a couple out and placed them on the bread board.

I stood up and stepped forward. I held my breath. I sneaked my hand around her waist and cradled her stomach.

"Listen," she said, as she smeared the bread with butter. "I'm grateful that you helped me home but the sandwich is all you get from me. Jesus, you poms are always on heat." She did not seem alarmed by the sudden embrace and did not care enough to push me away. I took her hand in my fist and tightened her fingers around the knife.

She wriggled like a pig but she was so drunk she did not have the strength to resist. The bread turned scarlet. She fell gurgling against the table and slowly capsized. I could not lift her into a chair so I left her on the floor. I tidied her hair and arranged her hands. She made a lovely picture in her party frock.

While I knelt there and admired the fallen Marlene, I had a sudden desire to reach out and touch her breasts. Her dress had been torn from one shoulder and was left hanging by a thread, leaving one breast exposed. It was a heavy, luminous globe that I wanted to cradle and weigh in my rubber hands. I crawled closer and hesitated before the object of my temptation. I had rarely experienced such an erotic melancholy and the sensation frightened me. I drew my eyes away from the breast and stared at her neck. Ah, the sight of her breast had made me tremble with lust but when I stared at her neck I turned faint at the sight of blood. It was the most beautiful colour, bright and clear as wine. I leaned forward and pressed my mouth against her neck, tasted her blood on my tongue. I could not resist. I was overcome by desire. I wanted to plant a single kiss, the kiss of death, against her skin. The blood tasted warm and dark in my mouth.

It was dangerous to linger so long in her room, I knew I must gather my wits and escape, but Marlene held a deadly fascination. She reminded me of Wendy Figg and, for that reason alone, I wanted to take her home. There was a fresh pack of film in the Polaroid and I decided to use it. I was in a fever of excitement. I rushed to the cupboard where Marlene had taken the knife and rummaged there until I found a pair of scissors. Then I knelt beside the sleeping beauty and cut away her party frock. I worked down its entire length and peeled it away from her body.

She was magnificent. A fat and gleaming dolphin stranded on the dusty carpet. She rumbled, deep in her throat, as she cooled and it set her dimpled belly aquiver. The rumble rose and popped her mouth, escaping in a gentle sigh. I took another photograph and then considered moving her into a more dignified pose. She was nearly as big as Figg but I managed to drag her against the wall and prop her into a sitting position. I placed her hands in her lap and then reached for the camera. But as I raised the Polaroid to my eye I saw her collapse and topple forward, hiding her face between her hands. She collapsed from the shoulder to the thigh in a series of thick creases until she looked like a ruined pile of pastry. So I pulled her upright, found some pillows and propped her among them. I wanted her to look beautiful. I twisted and tweaked the pillows until she was comfortable, her shoulders square and her belly balanced on her knees. On the table, beside the scarlet bread, stood a pot of flowers. I picked one of the flowers and poked it gently behind her ear. Then I placed her hands on her hips and shot the film. There are many women in my collection but Marlene looked the most handsome in death. She was smiling. The blood glittered in a necklace at her throat.

Most of my victims have been women. I did not plan it this way. Women are natural victims. When a man is threatened with violence he will shrink back and prepare to defend himself. When a woman is threatened with violence she will stumble forward to embrace it. A man will snarl and lash out with his feet and fists. A woman will cover her face in her hands. Blood seeps sluggishly from men. Blood pours joyfully from women. I cannot fathom the reasons for this difference in the animal. But, it is true, women are natural victims. As I began to collect material for the history of conjuring I saw clearly how all the great magicians had always used women as victims in their most violent and dangerous feats. They had thrown knives and pointed pistols at them, set fire to them, drowned them and buried them alive, locked them up and knocked them down; while the women themselves stood smiling, smiling in their stockings and sequins patiently waiting for the applause. And although, I must admit, I was unable to bring my own female assistants back from the dead at the end of each performance, I liked to think of myself as part of a long and honourable tradition.

The history was already taking shape in my head. I worked a little each day, sifting through the material and making notes in a large red exercise book until the pages were crammed with paradox and phantasm. It was going to be a long history. Frank would be proud of me. I grew to love the smell of the old theatre programmes I had collected, the dusty, crumbling texture of the ancient conjurer's encyclopedia, the spiral shavings as I cut my pencils with a penknife, the soft scratching sound of the pencils on paper and the loose, grey shape of each word as it squirmed free between my fingers. Sometimes I became so consumed by the simple physical pleasure of the work that I sat writing until dawn or fell asleep with my head in a book.

Nurse Jane phoned me at polite intervals and sometimes we would meet and go walking together along the Serpentine in Hyde Park. We sucked peanuts and held hands. Sprawled beside me in the grass she would ask questions about the history, clucking in sympathy or chuckling with admiration, depending upon my recent progress. Encouraged by her enthusiasm, I took my exercise book walking with me one afternoon and read passages aloud. When I asked her opinion, Nurse Jane laughed and kissed my mouth.

On the 2nd July – in memory of the Dusseldorf Vampire who met his executioners on that day – I went out and killed again. It wasn't easy and I took some foolish risks. But I had woken that morning from the most provocative dream of the mighty Marlene and spent the day in a restless and intoxicated mood. I could not write and nothing could have prevented me from exercising my skill with the knives that night. I felt as mad as a Moonie.

I waited until about nine o'clock when dusk had fallen, before I set out with my bag of tricks. But while I was sneaking down the stairs I heard someone move in the shadows behind me and a hand touched my shoulder. I nearly screamed.

"Good evening," said a familiar voice.

I turned to find Johnson Johnson standing on the stairs in his dressing gown. He was simpering and wringing his hands together.

"I wonder if you could help me," he said.

"What's wrong?" I asked suspiciously.

"It's my mother," he said, wiping his hands on his hair, "She's running a fever and she needs some ice cream to cool her down. It's nothing serious. But she says the ice cream helps damp down the pain."

"Well, I don't know . . ."

"Ah, I'm sorry – I thought you were going out somewhere," he said archly. He was staring, without expression, at my bag of murder weapons.

"Yes, I was going for a drive," I said as I tightened my grip on the bag.

"It wouldn't take a moment to stop at a supermarket. She doesn't like strawberry but any other flavour . . . no, she doesn't like nuts . . . but any other flavour, except toffee. Strawberry, toffee and nuts."

"But I might be gone for some time," I protested.

Johnson Johnson smiled and wagged his hands. "That's no problem. Whenever it suits you to come home. It's a great kindness."

"But the ice cream will melt."

"Oh, no, the supermarket will wrap it in paper for you if you explain."

"I don't know if I have my wallet on me," I whined in desperation.

But nothing could save me. Johnson Johnson stuffed money into my hand and smiled his hideous smile. I could have murdered him.

It isn't difficult to find a late night ice cream – there are half a dozen different places within walking distance of the house – but it seemed impossible, that evening, to buy anything that wasn't laced with strawberry sauce or sprinkled with nuts. I tried everywhere, ransacking freezers and interrogating checkout girls, but I might have been searching for candied larks' tongues.

Finally I had to drive as far as the Edgware Road where I managed to buy a bucket of chocolate chip surprise in a little supermarket owned by a Turk with one eye. It took me some time to find it, scratching and prising my way down through the fish and the cats' meat until I had reached the bottom of the freezer. And there, half frozen into the machine, was a single bucket of chocolate chip surprise waiting for me to take it home. It had been waiting there for a very long time because the Turk had to use a knife to hack it out of the ice. I was so happy when he finally broke the bucket free and gave it to me I could have kissed him. But I let him cheat on the price instead.

I found an old newspaper on the back seat of the car and wrapped the precious ice cream into a bundle. It was safe. I didn't need to hurry home – the cargo would not thaw for hours – so I began to drive north towards Regents Park.

I am not a disagreeable man. If we were introduced I hope you would think me a gentleman. I am not a monster. There is nothing extraordinary in my manner or approach. We may have already sat together on a train or passed each other in the street. You would not remember. But if we were introduced and you could bring yourself to accept the facts of my singular passion, we might become friends. I am an honest and dependable friend. The business of the ice cream, however, had prodded a raw nerve. I hated Johnson Johnson and his wretched mother. They had a trick of trapping me whenever I set out deliberately to avoid them.

Driving slowly through the quiet streets, I tried to restore my good humour and turned my thoughts again to murder. If I was lucky I could manage a quick one before the ice cream melted. It was a hot, moonlit night and the air was filled with flying insects. They rattled against the windscreen of the car as I drove and fell at my feet when I walked. I broke into a house in Primrose Hill and finished two old ladies. They died sweetly and without a struggle. When they saw me standing in the room they did not seem surprised. They looked as if they had been expecting me and, trembling, tried to rise from their chairs. Their hands were dry as dead leaves. Their faces were ancient and whiskery.

"Are you the doctor?" one of them asked.

"Yes," I said, "Please, sit down and make yourselves comfortable."

"You don't *look* like the doctor," one of them said confidentially.

"I've been sick," I said. I dumped my bag on the floor and rummaged through it, searching for the sharpest knives. "How long does ice cream take to melt?"

"An hour?" asked the first old lady.

"Two hours?" inquired the second old lady.

"I don't know," I said. There were several cats in the room watching me with their crafty, luminous eyes. I wondered idly if I could catch them.

"Do you *want* some ice cream?"

"No, thank you," I said as I gently administered the blades.

When I was finished with the ladies I set out to explore the house. There were photographs everywhere, on the walls, on the tables and cupboards and shelves. The pictures were so old they had turned brown and faded at the edges. The portraits were no more than rust-coloured ghosts in silver frames. Hundreds of dead faces staring at me from every direction. I suppose some of the photographs must have included the old women as children but I could not have recognised them. And there was a peculiar smell in the house. Carpets rotted with dust. Woodwork riddled with worm. Cats. Newspapers. I don't know. But I found I could not blow the smell from my nostrils. It seemed to cling to my clothes and hair.

It was while I was climbing the stairs that a terrible thought came to me. I went cold. What if she didn't like chocolate? If she didn't like toffee there was every chance she wouldn't like chocolate chip surprise. Perhaps I should search for some orange or vanilla on the way home?

In one of the bedrooms I found a bowl of irises. I took a knife and cut the heads from the stems. In another bedroom I discovered a canary in a bamboo cage but when I opened the little door and put in my hands the bird flew against the bars, shrieking and shedding feathers, and I could not catch it. Finally, I emptied the cage through the bedroom window and let the bird fly out to feed on the soft-bellied insects of the night.

I took a Polaroid of the old ladies as they sat quietly slumped in their chairs. Marlene, in death, had appeared to be sleeping. This strange pair of maids looked as alert in death as they had in life. They were so old that the distance between life and death was too narrow to be measured. As I waited patiently for the print to dry, a telephone began to ring. It was a strange sound in the land of the dead and I did not answer it.

I decided against going in search of orange or vanilla but I had to leave the premises for the sake of the chocolate and I drove home as fast as I dared under the circumstances. When I reached Warwick Square I retrieved the newspaper bundle from the back seat. The newspaper was sodden and peeled away in limp shreds. I held the bucket in my hands and gave it an experimental shake. There was a heavy splashing sound and to my dismay, when I prised up the lid, it threw a brown fleck of sludge over my fingers. The ice cream was ruined!

As I locked the car I glanced nervously at my watch. It was past midnight. If I was lucky, Johnson Johnson would be asleep. I liked to think of him curled up like a gnome in the arms of his mother, a thumb to plug his mouth and a ribbon for his hair. Gently, without a sound, I placed the little bucket of brown slops outside his door and tiptoed upstairs to safety.

"Goodnight," whispered Johnson Johnson as I fumbled with my key in the door, "And thank you."

The morning after the murders I slept late. I crawled from the sheets with my eyes full of glue when the telephone rang. I managed to pick it up and wheeze heavily into the receiver. But before I could say a word an angry voice was snapping at my ear.

"I called you last night."

"Oh, I'm sorry . . ." The alarm bells were deafening. I began mentally to hose the blood from the walls, drag corpses into cupboards and throw knives into buckets of soapy water. Clean and empty. No fingerprints. But where had I gone last night? Why hadn't I heard the telephone? I fell asleep in the bath. No, that wasn't an answer. I had a headache and took a dose of pain-killers. Dorothy suddenly cartwheeled into my thoughts. When life gets difficult fall down and play dead. No. It was too complicated. There was Johnson Johnson and the ice cream. Yes. But who goes shopping for ice cream in the dead of night?

"I phoned three times. I was worried," Jane complained.

"Yes, . . . I went out for some fresh air."

"Until past midnight?"

"Yes, it *was* late," I confessed.

There was a pause.

"Is everything all right?" she asked.

"Yes, of course, I just needed to get some fresh air. I feel trapped sometimes," I said.

"Why didn't you call me? We could have done something together."

"I wasn't feeling very happy. I didn't want to bore you with my problems."

"What are you talking about, William? What problems?"

"No problems, Jane. I just felt restless."

"Are you sure everything is all right?" she asked again.

Yes, of course everything is all right. Everything is fine. I just slipped out for a few hours and butchered a couple of old women the other side of town. Cut out their liver and fed it, hot and twitching, into my mouth. It happens all the time. It's nothing to worry about. I've never felt better in my life.

"Yes, I'm fine," I said.

"I called to invite you over for supper tomorrow night – unless of course you'd prefer to be alone," she added with lingering resentment.

"Supper would be lovely," I said, "Thank you."

"Nine o'clock. The house will be empty . . ."

"Can I bring anything?"

"A bottle of wine?"

"Yes. Anything else?"

"A toothbrush," she said and rang off.

I had been caught! Despite all the artistry and caution I had exercised in my brilliant career, I had been caught by Nurse Jane. I was no longer free to take my knives on midnight walks. Nurse Jane was watching! But it was the prospect of taking my toothbrush to supper that really alarmed me. I had learned to master some extraordinary tricks in my time – Dorothy had helped me rehearse them – but the simple, most natural task that Jane would expect from me had never been performed. I could go and ask Frank to explain but he wouldn't believe me and, anyway, I did not want to share Jane with him. I would have to manage alone.

The following afternoon I went out and bought a bottle of champagne and a new toothbrush. I sat in the bath and scrubbed my skin to a shine. I shaved twice and polished my nails. It took hours to prepare myself. I wanted everything to be perfect. It's an important moment in a man's life.

At eight-thirty I drove down to Chelsea and parked on a corner of the street. I sat there for a little while, trying to compose myself and raise my courage by sketching lewd portraits of a naked Nurse Jane in my head. Nurse Jane among the pillows, wearing nothing but freckles and a satisfied smile. But, somehow, everything between her shoulders and her knees was beyond my imagination. I was too frightened to take off her frock. I tried to reassure myself with the memory of Dorothy, rolled into a ball and tied with knots. But the memory only led to a view of myself, naked and struggling, under the ropes and it failed to lend me confidence. Finally, prepared if necessary to tell Jane that I had forgotten the toothbrush and couldn't stay the night, I swung the bottle of champagne under my arm and strolled towards the house.

As soon as I had reached the front door it swung open and Jane was standing there, smiling and reaching for my arm.

"I was watching from the window," she said as she led me up the stairs to her rooms. She was wearing a white shirt and a grey pleated skirt. The skirt opened and closed in a fan as she walked.

"Sit down," she said.

The room was small and immensely cluttered. There were two chairs with ragbag cushions, an old table with carved legs, a TV set on a wooden stool, a bench supporting fifty kinds of potted plant, a standard lamp, an electric fire and shelves of books, bowls of dried flowers, boxes of sea shells, more books, a child's stuffed bear with no ears, framed photographs, more books, and finally, across the far side of this crowded obstacle course, a beaded curtain hid a little kitchen.

The kitchen was no bigger than a wardrobe, yet Jane had managed to prepare steaks as big as dinner plates, green salad, scarlet salad, baked potatoes and hot fruit puddings.

"I hope you're hungry," she said.

I opened the champagne; which was warm and foamed over my shoes. We ate supper with the slow, deliberate movements of strangers, smiling often but speaking seldom. My palms were damp and my throat felt so tight I could barely swallow. My blood was sizzling like sherbet.

When we had finished we sat in our chairs and covered the distance between us with words.

"I'm sorry if I sounded angry on the phone yesterday," she said. She crossed her legs and the skirt that she wore slid away from her knee.

"It was more like an interrogation than an invitation," I said.

"It was silly – but I was worried. I thought something terrible might have happened to you."

"What?"

"Well – I don't know – anything." She stroked her knee, running her hand down the length of her calf and scratching at her ankle. She was barefoot and the toes seemed very long and white.

"I know . . . I'm sorry," I said. There had been one night, not so long ago, when I had tried to telephone Jane and found the line engaged for hours and grew jealous and afraid that she might have another lover and so, when she finally answered, I could not speak but rang off as soon as I heard her voice.

"If I didn't care about you . . ." she said and her voice trailed away. She uncrossed her legs and pulled at the skirt, fanning the pleats with her fingers, revealing a lazy glimpse of her thigh. The movement of the skirt stirred a warm and perfumed draught around the room.

"Thank you for supper," I said gently.

"Thank you for the champagne," she said, smiling and wiping the hair from her face. "It was very extravagant."

And then there was silence while we both struggled to find more conversation and I wanted to stretch out and touch her but did not have the courage. I should not have been so eager to thank her for the evening. It might have sounded as if I was ready to leave without so much as a kiss goodnight.

"Are you tired?" she asked suddenly.

I nodded. Yes. But I did not understand the question. Should I put on my coat or take off my shirt?

Jane stood up and walked behind my chair, forking her fingers through my hair and making me shiver with pleasure.

"Did you remember to bring your toothbrush?"

"Yes," I said, anxiously searching my pockets. I pulled it out and held it up for her inspection. The bristles had collected all the hairs, loose threads and crumbs from the bottom of my pocket. I picked them off gingerly.

Jane smiled and stepped into the kitchen. The curtain clattered and she was gone. I sat in the chair and stared at the bookshelves, waiting for my instructions. I stood up and peered at the potted plants, waiting for Jane to creep through the curtain naked and wrap her arms around my waist. Whatever doubts I might have entertained about this intimate encounter were already evaporated. My lack of experience only served to heighten my excitement and curiosity. I waited for the moment when Jane returned wearing nothing but freckles. I waited but nothing happened. Finally I pushed my head through the curtain and peeped into the kitchen. It was empty. I crept inside and discovered that it led immediately into a narrow corridor and at the end of the corridor lay another room.

I pushed open the door and stepped into the room. I was confused by the darkness. A single candle burned in one corner and its light fluttered madly among the shadows. I screwed up my face and stared blindly into the gloom. Slowly the shadows began to brighten and fill with colour. There was a writing desk and a chest of drawers. A small chair. Against one wall a wooden bed. Upon the bed Nurse Jane was curled among the pillows. She had taken off her skirt and folded it neatly over the chair. Her legs were drawn up tightly against her chest. Her hair sparkled in the candlelight but her face was hidden in darkness.

At first I thought she was asleep. But as my eyes grew familiar with the light I saw that she was not sleeping but awake and watching me. After a moment she began to unfurl herself and rolled slowly onto her back, propping her head and shoulders against the pillows. Her arms settled into the folds of the sheets and were lost but she drew up her legs and parted them, gazing between them as I stepped forward.

"I thought you were lost," she whispered.

"I was waiting," I said casually as I dragged off my clothes.

"I'm ready," she whispered.

I reached out my arm and touched her foot with my fingertips. The long toes arched. My eyes stole from her foot, over the motionless leg to the darkness between her thighs. Her limp and passive beauty filled me with despair. I didn't know where to begin.

I withdrew my arm and prepared to step back from the bed but she, rising, caught hold of my hand and drew me down among the pillows. We rolled together in the sheets and then she was sitting astride me with her knees locked hard against my hips. I stared up at her in amazement. Her body was slender and very pale. Her hair tumbled into her eyes but she did not brush it away. I picked at the buttons of her shirt until her breasts swung heavy and loose above my face.

I cupped one breast so gently in my palm I felt the nipple wriggle as it hardened in my fingers. Then she sank down upon her elbows and I covered her breasts with my mouth, teasing the nipples, forcing them erect, making them shine. She pulled away suddenly and sat above me with her spine stretched and her eyes glittering.

She ran her fingers slowly between my legs and, with all the dexterity of a magician, charmed that shy and crumpled member of the audience into a plump and eager assailant. She rolled it against her palms for a few moments, gripped it firmly at the base, as if she were grasping a dagger, and thrust it smoothly into her belly. She swallowed it with a single stroke and squirmed comfortably. I tried to move within and without her body, but my arms were held against the sheets and my legs were restricted by her weight. Again and again she plunged the dagger into her body, moaning and thrashing her face with her hair, while I could only gasp for breath and watch her, startled and alarmed by the violence of her desire.

"Does it hurt?" I whispered.

"It kills me," she moaned. And it was true, our ecstasies resembled the sighs and whispers of death.

Mine was a sudden death. I pulled her face towards me and thrust my tongue between her teeth, so that I might know the thrill of this double penetration and the life rushed from me with a great shudder. I fell back into the pillows, disappointed. But the dagger was strong and planted deep. Nurse Jane continued to rise and plunge, oblivious to my wasted condition. And I remember thinking, I am here sprawled naked beneath the woman I love, who is also naked but lovely, and burning with an exquisite heat, hair flying, breasts bouncing, eyes closed, mouth open, teeth flashing in the candlelight and I don't believe it. And – although I don't believe it – I must forget nothing and hoard this memory against the day I am withered and old and alone. I traced the shape of her breasts with my hands, counted her ribs with my fingertips, committed her shape to memory. I watched her face, amazed by her concentration and ferocity, hoping to catch the supreme moment of her own capitulation. I watched her face but when she gave up the struggle she cried out as if she were suffocating, and I could not tell the pleasure from the pain.

We did not speak. We lay tangled in the ruined bed and fell asleep. When I woke again it was barely dawn. The room was hot. A pale wash of light seeped through the window. An alarm clock purred quietly to itself beside the bed. Jane was turned away from me, her body curled into a clenched fist and her breath reduced to a hiss. I slipped carefully from the sheets. My neck ached and my bones creaked. I clambered into my clothes and stood for a moment, staring at the foot of the bed. Jane was still asleep. I was tempted to try and peel back the sheet to steal a glimpse of her drowsy breasts or plant a kiss on her shoulder. But I turned instead and tiptoed away.

I wanted to escape before she woke up and offered me breakfast. I didn't want her to catch me with my face swollen from sleep, my hair in strings and my breath poisoned. I wanted the night to remain extraordinary and untouched by daylight.

And that is how it remained for, although I sent her flowers in the afternoon, when we met again we did not speak of that night. It had become a dream to haunt me.

It was the first week in August when the *Daily Mirror* published the special feature on my work. It was very interesting. They had managed to obtain photographs of my every victim. There were old wedding portraits, blurred holiday snapshots, ugly passport pictures, the faces filled half a page. There were even one or two faces I did not recognise and, counting carefully, knew I could not have murdered. But it was an education.

I learned, for the first time, the names of my victims and something of their lives. Patsy's client, I discovered, had been John Horace, the publisher. The two old ladies had been the Hornet Sisters, famous long ago for a musical comedy act. There were several minor celebrities on the list. It's funny but I have never had the desire to kill a president or a pope, the pistol waved above the crowd, the screams of the limousines and the bawling guards. There's no art to the public assassination.

I had kept a scrapbook from the beginning. But I was especially proud of my *Daily Mirror* page – it was something special. Here at last the full extent of my work went on public view. There was even a map of London with each murder marked as a small black star. And a long paragraph on the special squad of detectives who were said to be devoted to my capture and conviction. The team included senior police officers and a forensic scientist.

Until that time I had appeared in the press only briefly and under a variety of pseudonyms. But the police had finally recognised the touch of the master in the application of the blades and the attitude of the corpses. The victims, declared one of the police officers in an unguarded moment, had been killed quickly and neatly. The man they wanted had all the skill of a butcher.

I had often wondered how the police viewed my work. Once or twice I had even been tempted to phone them and report one of my murders while the blood was still warm; standing on the street at the scene of the crime, watching them arrive with their notebooks and their cameras eager to examine the corpse. I have always wondered about the nature of their loathsome work as they kneel to the carrion, prodding and poking in search of signs of violation. I transform the living into the dead with a kiss of the knife and artful fingers while they wrench the dead limb from limb with morbid fascination. I wonder if we share the same addiction.

The next day my new name appeared on the front page of every national newspaper, the Butcher, the Butcher, as if shouting the name of death might arrest its career. Men walked into police stations claiming to be the Butcher and tried to confess to my crimes. There were hoax telephone calls to local radio stations and several Butchers wrote letters to the newspapers threatening violence.

The clamour lasted for nearly a month and then it went wrong. One morning I was the most dangerous killer since the Black Death. Women buried their faces in their skirts, men slipped penknives under their pillows, children were forbidden to walk in the streets. The next morning the Butcher had been arrested and the police were already making guest appearances on the early TV news. I couldn't believe it. The Butcher had hardly been given time to sharpen his knives. And now it was finished.

The nation rejoiced. The newspaper editors managed to find a photograph of the killer and ran special Butcher souvenir editions. The TV producers tried to thread all their old news reports together and run Butcher specials. A crowd gathered outside Paddington Green Police Station where the Butcher was rumoured to be chained in a cell. The *Sunday Times*, that same week, published ten thousand words on the murders – the moral and political significance of the psychopath in society – and even managed a couple of paragraphs on the man who confessed to the crimes.

His name was Morris Hudson, an unemployed painter and decorator who lived in an attic in Brixton. He was arrested for trying to steal a car and immediately confessed to the Butcher murders. It was madness. He was only seventeen years old. He didn't look bright enough to tie a knot in his own bootlaces, let alone conduct a series of rather artistic murders. But the police were holding him and the police must have had their reasons.

It was a problem. If I could resist the knives it was more than likely that poor Morris Hudson would be found guilty of the Butcher's crimes. If I killed again the idiot would be set loose and the game could continue forever. I wasn't tired of the sport. I had no regrets. And yet, here was a unique opportunity to hang up my gloves and retire from the profession. I could finish my history of conjuring. I could allow my love for Jane to become a comfortable habit, an opium to cloud my memory and help me finish my life in peace. If I could resist the knives.

I tried to dismiss Morris Hudson as a victim of his own imagination. I had found a book about a Victorian theatre of magic called the Egyptian Hall and I set about reading it. All manner of monsters and miracles were presented on the stage of the Egyptian Hall. The Scorpion Woman, the Invisible Boy, Doctor Leech and General Tom Thumb. But none of them held the same morbid fascination as Morris Hudson. I found it difficult to concentrate, I laboured over the pages and could not gather my thoughts. It was impossible.

I abandoned the idea of reading and washed the windows instead. When I had finished I felt better and searched for something else that would waste my energy and help me sleep. I scrubbed out the kitchen but my old rubber gloves sprang a leak and I had to throw them away and walk down to Woolworth and find a new pair to finish the job. I chose a bright yellow pair with long, sporty sleeves that reached almost to my elbows. The palms were coated with thousands of tiny nipples which, according to the packet, gave them extra grip on small and slippery objects. I could not resist holding a knife in my fist, to test the clutch of the nipples on steel, and before I knew what had happened I had packed my tool bag with the gloves and the knives.

I hid in the bedroom with Hubert's Conjuring Encyclopedia but when I turned the pages a Polaroid fell out and fluttered to the floor at my feet. When I picked it up I saw Marlene peeled neat as a banana, with her frock split open from the shoulders to the thighs and a splash of colour against her neck.

It was getting dark. I phoned Nurse Jane to beg her to lead me from temptation. A walk along the Embankment. A plate of Chinese noodles. Anything that would keep me from sitting and thinking alone. But the telephone rang and was not answered. Ten minutes later I was driving into North London.

I chose one of those big, expensive apartment blocks in St John's Wood. It looked like a Victorian hospital with gold trimmings. There was a complicated security lock on the door but someone had left the door unlatched and I managed to slip inside without being challenged. While the Butcher was held in handcuffs the rich widows of St John's Wood felt safe enough to leave their cages open. I quickly found the fire stairs and clambered to the roof. I was hoping to find an isolated attic where I might work my mischief beyond earshot of inquisitive neighbours. But I found, instead, a large penthouse that ran the length of the flat roof and was approached along a short gravel path, flanked by pots of ornamental shrubs. It was a most peculiar sight and seemed to float in the night sky with nothing but a distant church spire to link it with the earth. When it rained or when there was fog, the place must have floated remote as a Pacific island, forgotten and invisible to its neighbours. It was the perfect spot for a murder.

I tiptoed in and out of the potted shrubs, hoping to peer through the penthouse windows, but the blinds had been drawn and I could see nothing. So I took a deep breath and rang the bell. There was a rattle of chains and the door flew open.

He was a big man in a red silk dressing-gown and patent leather shoes. He looked like an ancient heavyweight boxer who had spent his career having his nose broken and his mouth split open in a fairground tent. His face had been battered into a shapeless mask, hard as leather and mottled with scars. At a distance you might have thought he had a stocking pulled over his head. His grey hair had been shaved to a stubble so that his ears seemed to grow naked from his skull like a pair of sickly truffles.

"Good evening," I said with a smile.

"Who are you?" he asked in mild surprise. He peered around in the dark as if waiting for someone to arrive and introduce us in a formal manner.

"Is Benny here?" I inquired.

"Who?" he asked.

"Benny," I said, "He promised me he would be here."

"You've got the wrong address."

"No," I said, "Benny promised he would be here tonight."

"There's no one here called Benny."

"Yes," I insisted, "He said he'd be here by eight o'clock."

"I've been alone all evening," he said flatly, "I don't know who you are and I've never heard of Benny. Goodnight."

"You're alone?" I asked incredulously.

"Yes."

I smiled and pushed him backwards through the door. He spluttered and swore at me but he was too alarmed to offer any resistance. He fell back into the room and I kicked the door closed with my foot.

The room looked as if it had been assembled by a designer who specialised in small brothels for syphilitic kings. One wall was hung with pink mirrors set in flamboyant gilt frames. Another wall was covered in gloomy oil paintings of Victorian nudes with buttocks the colour of butchers' lard. Beside the door a marble table with legs of twisted antlers supported a bowl of peacock feathers. In the far corner a naked blackamoor held an electric lamp shaped like a bowl of tropical fruit. And in the centre of the room, set upon a low wooden stage, stood a grand piano.

"Sit down," I said gently.

He walked across the room and sat down at the piano. He tapped out a little tune with one finger. I knelt down and opened my bag of tools. I peeled on my new rubber gloves, watching him and trying hard to ignore the extraordinary surroundings. I selected a knife, weighed it in the palm of my hand, stood up and walked to the piano. The man in the dressing-gown did not move or make a sound. He just sat there and watched me approach.

I thought, he is frozen by fear. I shall raise my hand and stroke his ear with the knife. He will fall into his music and be gone. But when I reached the piano he shook his head and smiled.

"Listen, I'm a rich man," he said cheerfully, "You don't have to hurt me. I like you. You've got spirit. I'll give you whatever you want. Paintings. Jewels." He raised his hand and gestured about the room, inviting me to choose a prize.

His voice, in contrast to his face, was smooth and precise. When he talked he flicked his tongue in and out like a lizard. It was very sinister and I thought, yes, he is a huge reptile in a dressing-gown, slow but cunning and waiting for the moment to catch my fingers in his jaws. I was frightened, of course I was frightened, for there is a moment in any confrontation when it is not yet decided who shall be victor and who shall fall victim. He could have cracked my ribs or broken my neck. He could have pulled a pistol from his dressing-gown and blown off my head. Anything might have happened.

"I'm not interested," I said with a smile.

"Money," he suggested. "I'll give you money. A suitcase full of money." The lizard flicked his tongue and watched me with a yellow eye.

"No."

"Women. I could let you have women. Beautiful women. Hungry women. All colours. Whatever you want." Now it was his turn to smile as he sat and waited for my reply.

"No."

"Boys? You like boys? I understand. I'm a man of the world –I've enjoyed the odd boy myself. Whatever you want I'm prepared to give you without a struggle. Throw that knife away."

"Blood," I confessed.

"What?"

"I've come for your blood," I explained. I didn't want to frighten him, but he didn't seem to understand the situation.

"You need dope? My friend, I can help you. Allow me to make a phone call and I can put you out of your misery."

"You don't seem to understand. I've come to put an end to your misery," I said.

"You're making a mistake," he smiled, "You've got the wrong man."

"No," I shook my head sadly.

"You're crazy – I could give you anything," he complained.

I tried to spear a truffle with my knife but he threw back his head and the blade did not settle. Before I could recover my balance he had leapt from the piano and scuttled across the room. He tried to hide behind the blackamoor. The sash of his dressing-gown had worked loose and was trailing around his ankles.

"You can't kill me. I'm an old man," he shouted as I walked towards him, the knife in my fat rubber hand. I made a grab for his neck but he swerved aside and caught the blade in his shoulder. It clung like a fork in a knuckle of pork. He pushed past me and returned to the piano, felt the knife in his dressing-gown and began to rub his fingers in the blood, holding his fingers under his nose and sniffing them suspiciously.

"Try and see it another way," I suggested helpfully, "A neat hole behind your ear and you're gone. It's very peaceful. You're an old man – you should understand these things. There are some terrible ways to die. You could drown. That's horrible. Or smother in your pillows. That's nasty."

"Stop," he bawled as I followed him across the room. "You'll regret this tomorrow morning. Calm down and we'll have a drink."

I pulled another knife from my bag and tried again. But he was too fast for me and when I tried to puncture his neck the lizard swung away and took the blade in his chest.

"What would you like? Anything. Brandy? Champagne? Let's talk about this over a long, cold drink," he roared as he staggered from the stage towards a cocktail cabinet. He was beginning to resemble a pin cushion. I pulled another knife from the bag and followed him across the room.

"You wouldn't want to be much older," I said kindly, "Wetting the sheets and forgetting your name. Living on cabbage water and slops."

But as I stalked him the lizard turned suddenly with a bottle of champagne in his fist. He raised the bottle like a club and, rather than wait for me to reach him, flung it at me with a shout. He was a poor marksman. The bottle spun past and hit the blackamoor full in the face, cracking off her nose and the greater part of her jaw. The old lizard roared in pain as the blackamoor was hit. He ran towards her, snatched up the broken jawbone and began to nurse it in his hands.

"What have you done?" he blubbered as he peered at the shattered face. He scratched the brittle plaster with his fingernails and tried to press the fragments back into place. But he was too confused to solve the jigsaw and threw the piece at me in frustration.

"I'm sorry," I said.

But he ignored me. The injury received by his naked lamp bearer seemed to have unbalanced his mind. He staggered miserably around the room and then fell in a heap on the floor. For a moment I couldn't move but at last I forced myself forward and tried to find the courage to use another knife. I was so upset by the violence my hands were trembling. Finally I speared a truffle and he left the land of the living with a grunt of pain and a whistling sigh of relief.

Men are full of offal. They're crammed to bursting with pipes and tubes and entrails, heart, kidneys, liver and lights, tripe and chitterlings. When I was a child I used to think that my own body was like a butcher's carcass, hollow and clean with the vital organs hanging on threads, like Christmas presents, from the bones of my shoulders. But the human body is just a balloon full of hot and bubbling mud. Puncture them and they leak all over the carpet.

There was blood everywhere. Blood splashed on the door. Blood sprinkled along the piano keys. He had not merely run about in his fright – he had *smeared* his way across the room, painting his possessions with the stuff as it leaked from him. Perhaps he had hoped to collect it in a sponge when I was gone and squeeze it into his mouth. A pity to waste it. Perhaps he was simply afraid of staining the precioús carpet and preferred to wipe his hands on the walls. It was a gaudy spectacle. It suggested a violence far greater than anything I had inflicted and it upset me. I wanted to take a bucket of soapy water and wipe the room clean, tidy the cushions and polish the glass. But I decided to leave it alone, collected my bag and left the premises. Foolish to be arrested with a scrubbing brush in my hand.

It was not a very good example of my work to offer the authorities – it lacked my usual lightness of touch. But it served the purpose. Within a week the poor cuckoo who thought he was the Butcher had been winkled out of prison and thrown back onto the streets. I had taken one life and saved another. No one thanked me.

The morning after the murder I woke up with the sun in my eyes and the jangle of bells in my ears. I staggered from the bedroom and fell over my tool bag as I reached for the phone.

"Good morning," said Jane.

"I called you last night," I mumbled absently.

"What time?"

"Oh, about nine o'clock," I yawned. I was still hot and itching with sleep. I balanced on one leg, scratching my shin with my toes. My skin felt smothered in sand.

"I went out with a girlfriend," she said crisply, "And where were you?"

"I was here."

"Wrong."

"Yes, of course I was here," I insisted stubbornly.

"I phoned when we got home, around eleven."

"I must have been asleep."

"And you didn't hear the phone."

"That's right. I must have been dead to the world." I tried to laugh but my tongue felt swollen and glued to my teeth.

"How are you feeling today?" she inquired, and her voice went so cold I did not recognise her and felt suddenly frightened.

"Fine . . . I thought we might spend the evening together," I said slowly.

There was a pause. The silence between us filled with crackle and the far away music of other conversations.

"All right," she said at last, "I'll come over to your place."

"No. Let's go out somewhere," I said quickly. She had asked a dozen times but I couldn't risk inviting her into my rooms, picking through my papers, my scrapbooks, my photographs and knives. I couldn't risk it.

"Come here," she said simply, without bothering to argue with me and again I heard the unfamiliar coldness in her voice that was so disturbing.

"What time?"

"Whenever you're ready."

"Jane?"

"Yes?"

"What's wrong?"

"Nothing."

She rang off. I felt like I'd been hit with a telegraph pole. I went back to bed and tried to hide under the pillow. But I knew that it was finished. Gradually, perhaps without us even noticing the change, we had grown to depend on each other and if that dependence continued it was inevitable that, sooner or later, I would drag Jane into my secret world and force her to share my guilt. Something would go wrong. I was so anxious to disguise the truth that something, somehow, would go wrong. I couldn't keep Jane at arm's length for the rest of my life, forbid her to knock on my door or phone me whenever she wanted to talk.

When I managed at last to find the strength to get dressed I dragged myself into the bathroom and fed the razor with a new blade. I didn't have the courage to end the affair, I could only wait for Jane to feel hurt and angry enough to finish it for me. And what kind of choice was that, Mackerel Burton? None. Exactly. I splashed my face with hot water and smeared a dollop of shaving cream on my chin.

I kept telling myself, over and over, you were content before you lost your tooth and found a lover and you will be content again. The pain will flare and die and you will be able to forget. But I didn't believe it. My brain was collapsing between my ears and I believed in nothing but my own cowardice. The blade nicked my cheek and a bubble of soap filled with blood.

It was not just a question of losing a woman. If I wanted a woman I could take her by pointing a knife at her throat. At my command, women would run naked on their hands and knees, barking like dogs. I could paint lipstick targets on their backsides and throw eggs at them. Beneath the seductive influence of the knife a woman would bend over backwards, turn somersaults, to entertain me. But I did not want the tricks of some performing animal, smelling of hatred and fear. I wanted the only woman that the knives would not allow me and that was Nurse Jane. The bubble of blood fell from my cheek and made a splash against my collar.

I went down to Chelsea in the afternoon. The Thames was glossy as gravy and running high against the Embankment. Across the river Battersea Power Station was pumping smoke into an empty sky. I parked the car opposite Jane's house and she appeared on the doorstep before I had a chance to ring the bell. She was wearing a dressing-gown and a turban knotted from towels. The weight of the turban had pushed her ears flat against her head. She looked pale and miserable. I reached forward to kiss her but she turned away and walked upstairs. I followed her in silence. When we reached her rooms she closed the door and escaped into the little kitchen.

"Do you want a drink?" she called through the clatter of the bead curtain.

"Thank you," I said.

She returned with a half bottle of vodka and a carton of orange juice which she placed on the table beside me. Her neck appeared painfully brittle beneath the great volume of towels she carried on her head. She stood at the table and stared at the bottle for two or three seconds and then went in search of glasses. The seal on the vodka hadn't been broken and she must have bought it as an anaesthetic especially for the occasion.

"What's wrong?" I pleaded as she fiddled with the spout on the orange juice.

"You disappear – I phone you and you've disappeared," she said and thumped the carton on the table.

"I was asleep."

"I'm not talking about last night," she continued, turning to confront me at last. "I'm talking about all the other nights when I've phoned and you didn't answer."

"It's not true," I wailed.

"What is it that's so terrible you can't speak about it?" she begged.

"Nothing. Nothing," I shouted, shaking my head and slicing at the air with my fingers.

"There's another woman," she declared. Her voice was suddenly small and calm.

"No," I said. Yes, I thought, that is the only sensible explanation. I am married to a woman called death and she is a fierce and jealous mistress. Her eyes are full of opium and her kisses taste of blood.

"William," she said slowly, "You've got to tell me the truth."

"I'm married," I said softly, hardly daring to pronounce the words.

"What?"

"I'm married. Her name is Doris. We. . .we're not living together exactly but I think. . ."

"I don't believe it," she said. She shook her head and the turban began to unravel, toppled forward and fell in her eyes. She clawed at the towels and pulled them away. There were tears in her eyes and she wrenched at the smallest towel, rubbing it quickly over her face.

"I'm sorry. . .I can't help it," I whined.

"I don't believe it," she repeated. She sniffed ferociously and scratched at her scalp. Her hair was still wet and clung to her head in tight, glossy curls.

"I'm sorry," I whispered. This was a deliberate act of murder, but far more terrible than anything I had ever committed in the past, for this murder created living corpses, victims who would walk away and continue to feel the wound itching and burning without rest.

"Are there any children?"

"Yes. No. I don't know. I can't talk about it."

"William, tell me the truth. That's all I'm asking."

"I'm not married. Her name is Doris. We're going to live together as soon as we find a place."

"When the hell did you meet this woman?" she asked amazed. She had managed to make woman sound like an unknown species, a grotesque animal.

"Three years ago."

"So you knew – all the time – you knew that this wasn't going to mean a damn thing to you."

"Jane. . ." The floor between us was stretching at an alarming rate, pulling us apart so that even as I pushed out my hand to touch her I knew I could never reach across the distance. She was shrinking from me, her face growing hard and remote.

"Don't touch me," she hissed.

I sat down at the table and hid my face in my hands. My eyes burned. I couldn't see across the room.

"I'm sorry."

"Where does she live?"

"What difference does it make?" I groaned.

"I want to know."

"Hammersmith." No, not Hammersmith! That's a killing ground, try somewhere else, use your imagination.

"Hammersmith?" she echoed. It even sounded strange to Jane.

"I went there a few times – that's how we met," I said. I was building a phantom lover from the skin and bones of the dead, inventing a lovers' lane in a graveyard. It was horrible.

"Were you sleeping together?"

"I love you," I blubbered.

"Were you sleeping together?"

"Yes."

"Bastard."

"I love you," I sobbed.

"Leave me alone! Go to hell!" she snapped. She broke open the anaesthetic and poured herself a slug, draining the glass and coughing into the towel. The dressing-gown had fallen open and she fumbled with the belt.

If my story had been true I might have begged to be forgiven, slashed my wrists, abandoned the one called Doris and married Jane. If any of it had been true there might have been some hope of repairing the damage. But I was trying to save her from the Sandman and I could only hold my silence and pray that she would not ask any more difficult questions. If I hesitated, even for a moment, I would weaken and confess the terrible truth.

"I never meant to hurt you," I whispered.

She didn't answer but stood, exhausted, staring vacantly at the floor.

"Please," she whispered finally, "Please go away."

I stood up and wiped my face. I walked from the room, down the stairs and into the street, closing the door behind me.

I am the Sandman. I am the Butcher in soft rubber gloves. I am the acrobat called death. I am the fear in the dark. I am the gift of sleep. Psychiatrists write pompous papers on the significance of my crimes. Clairvoyants search for my face in their dreams. Schoolboys speculate on the tortures I am rumoured to inflict upon women. And yet I am a stranger. I am celebrated and I am unknown. I am hunted by everyone and visited by no one. When I sit in cafés the waiters ignore me. When I walk in the market the matrons jostle me. When I stand in the street the traffic sweeps past me.

While the newspapers cried for my blood I sat alone in my room and cried for Jane. I stayed at home for more than a week. Frank came to lend me a book and I tried to make him welcome, offer him tea and cakes, but I felt depressed and did not have the energy to talk to him.

"Have you seen the newspapers today?" he inquired cheerfully, spitting tea and crumbs at me.

"No. . ."

"A woman in Manchester claims she knows the name of the Butcher. God gave it to her in a dream and she wants to broadcast it on television."

"I'll watch out for it," I mumbled.

"I feel sorry for him," Frank continued.

"Why?" I said. "He's a killer."

"Yes, but now he's a hunted man. It's becoming a national sport. Hunt the Butcher. Imagine how it must feel to be so mad and so alone."

"It will soon be finished," I said without conviction.

"Yes, I think you're right. They'll either catch him or he'll kill himself."

It was almost too much for me. There was nothing left to be said and I finished my tea in complete silence. Frank lingered for nearly half an hour, then took some books from my shelves and crept away.

There was something about Frank that fascinated me. He was an educated man. He spoke several languages and had travelled around the world. He knew so much about people and yet, despite his knowledge, he was prepared to forgive them anything. He could forgive them their cruelty and stupidity as if they were just boisterous children in a nursery school. He loved them. He made excuses for them. It's hard to believe but Frank always managed to find something good in people.

Sometimes, when he stared at me with his strange bright eyes, I thought he must be able to stare clean through me and see everything. There was a wrinkle at the corner of his mouth that gave him a vague and weary smile as if he were amused at what he saw. A glimpse of that smile made me nervous and I would turn away from him, pretend to search for a book or a packet of biscuits. But now I wanted to discard the old deceit and tell him the truth about myself.

I wanted to call him back and confess everything. I wanted to share my secret. I thought, he will sit in the chair beside the window and we will discuss the Sandman as if we were discussing a favourite book. He will nod his head from time to time to let me know he understands. We'll share a bottle of wine and the pain in my head will dissolve and be gone. He will not shrink from me in disgust. He is an educated man. He will accept the facts of death in my life. But I knew my confession would only lead to his murder and I kept my mouth pressed shut.

It was during the worst days of this loneliness that my mother died. The hospital sent me a telegram. She died suddenly and with a great deal of shouting early one morning while a nurse was feeding her breakfast. She had always hated hospital food and I think, towards the end, she had grown tired of searching for my father. She was old and bitter and full of venom.

Her death marked a most dismal episode in my life. I was an intimate friend of death, but nonetheless, when it dragged away my mother, struggling and shouting abuse, it also took a part of me. It cut away my family and my history and left me with nothing but myself. I found myself remembering, with painful clarity, the years I had spent in the old hotel. I remembered again my attic kingdom, the bed with its shallow wooden walls to prevent me from falling out of my dreams and the giant dolls my mother had sewn from rags. I remembered the smell of breakfast in my mother's cardigans and the shape of her face, plump as a speckled egg. I wept for these memories and found that I was not merely mourning the death of my mother but the death of myself as a child.

Dorothy and Archie took me home and helped me arrange the funeral. Dorothy was brisk and cheerfully efficient but Archie seemed stricken with grief and could not be comforted. He borrowed misfortunes wherever he could find them and seemed to almost rejoice in them. He hardly knew the old lady and yet he wept as if she were his own sister.

"It's terrible news," he said, shaking his great head miserably and holding my hand in his fists, "Terrible news. I still can't believe it."

"It was a shock," I admitted.

"If only we had known," he grieved, "If only we had known she was so sick we would have gone to visit her at Christmas.

We could have taken her some turkey breasts."

"No one knew," I said, "It was very sudden."

"You mustn't blame yourself," said Dorothy soothingly. She was looking at me but I think she was talking to Archie.

The funeral was a simple affair. There were no flowers and Dorothy and Archie served as the only mourners. Dorothy looked beautiful in black stockings. She held my arm thoughout the service and whispered sympathies in my ear.

It was a huge cemetery, full of carved Victorian virgins swooning over blocks of Italian marble. I remember thinking, the Victorians must have enjoyed their funerals. The sepulchral horses straining at the weight of the cut-glass hearse, the fluttering crepe, the muffled drums, the weepers pressed against the glittering sarcophagus. The Victorians knew exactly how to die in public. Mourners were two a penny and rented by the dozen. A good funeral was a life's ambition and they slept with their burial money under their pillows. Now the cemetery was a wasteland, a forgotten city of ghosts. Gulls glided in the bright September sky. The earth smelt sour and damp.

When it was finished and we turned to leave I thought I saw the tall, narrow figure of Uncle Eno standing in the shelter of an elm tree in a corner of the cemetery. But when I beckoned to him he smiled thinly and walked quickly away through the gates.

I spent a few more days with Dorothy and Archie, watching television and eating slices of boiled ham. Archie was very pleased with his hams – they had appeared at some of the most distinguished funeral suppers in Europe – and he had spared no expense in honour of my mother. It was a magnificent measure of pig, spiked with cloves and glazed with molasses and juniper.

I was sitting watching a factory fire on the early evening news when Archie produced the mighty meat. He sat it down before me as if he were offering the head of John the Baptist. Dorothy poured a jug of cold cider and, as we prepared the table, we began to talk again of the funeral.

"She was very old," said Archie, waving a carving knife over the ham. The knife had an intricate ivory handle trimmed with silver lace.

I nodded and smiled and stared at the knife.

"She was very feeble in the head," said Dorothy kindly, holding a plate and watching the blade stroke the ham.

"She deserved to be set free from those years of suffering," said Archie, hooking the slice of ham on the tip of his blade and folding it onto the plate.

"It was the best thing that could have happened," said Dorothy, picking up the plate and rolling the ham between finger and thumb.

"It was no life inside that hospital," agreed Archie, "They made her live on sausage meat."

"I expect she was glad to be gone," murmured Dorothy, pinching the flute between her fingers and pushing it slowly into my mouth.

I chewed the ham gently, feeling it dissolve against my tongue.

"I should like to have seen her before she died," I said sadly.

"She wouldn't have recognised you, Mackerel," said Dorothy.

"She lived in a world of her own," said Archie.

We whispered and smiled and sucked at our fingers. Gradually, slice by slice, we cut away at the guilt and grief until there was nothing left of my mad, old mother but a gleaming ham bone on a blue china plate.

We did not speak of my mother again. The next day we slept late and in the afternoon Archie insisted on escorting me around the grounds of the house. I thought it was an odd whim but I agreed to walk with him.

At the back of the house was a vegetable patch. Dorothy was very proud of it, she pickled its fruits, bottled its vegetables and made wine from the remains. Everything seemed to grow in that vegetable patch. If you cared to sit quietly, with your back against the kitchen door and your legs folded neatly in front of you, you could hear the roots suck and pull at the scalp of the earth, potatoes creak and pumpkins explode with a wet roar. In the heart of the undergrowth, dark with shrubs and peppery with herbs, lay a stone pond of black water. If you threw a crust into it you might see an ancient goldfish the colour of marble rise slowly to the surface and stare at you sideways. I loved the garden. But Archie seemed to have no time for it and led me urgently away, over the lawns, to the far corner of the grounds. And there, in the shadow of the wall, he showed me a great blister in the turf.

It was an old Second World War air raid shelter. A brick cellar covered by an immense cushion of earth. I had seen them in the past, covered in brambles and stinking of drains. But this shelter had been restored to its original glory, the pit had been excavated and a bright metal door had been fitted to the entrance. Archie stood before it and beamed at me.

"It's an air raid shelter," I explained.

"Yes."

"It must be something of an historical monument – it's in very good condition," I said to please him.

"I'm rebuilding it," he said.

"What will you do with it when it's finished?" I asked.

He looked perplexed. "It's obvious," he said and cocked his head at me suspiciously, "When the war comes again we'll live in here. I'm having it fully equipped for survival against nuclear blast, fire storms, radiation and looters."

"It's very fine," I said.

"Yes. It's a fortress. We can live in here for weeks and weeks when the time comes."

"And what will you do when the war is finished?" I asked him.

"Why, we'll come out again," he said with a laugh.

"Yes, but what will you do after a nuclear war?"

He cocked his head again and frowned. "I don't understand," he said slowly.

"Well, there'll be nothing left," I said, waving my arm in the general direction of the rest of the world.

Archie shrugged. "Survival," he said, "That's the important thing. We have to survive."

I didn't argue with him. He seemed so proud of his brick burial mound. Poor Archie. Life in the slaughter houses had made him unreasonably afraid of death. He had coined a fortune from butchering life and here he was investing that fortune in a Pharoah's tomb, a man in search of eternal life.

"Can you handle a rifle?" he said casually as we walked back to the house.

"No," I said.

"That's a pity," he said thoughtfully and I knew he had decided against inviting me to share his bunker.

I drove back to London, happy to return to the noise of the city. But when I reached Victoria I was reluctant to climb the stairs and unlock the door to my rooms. I was surprised by my own apprehension. I did not expect to find the police waiting for me behind an upturned table, or threatening letters on the doormat. No. I expected to find the Sandman. I had left him waiting there while I went to attend my mother's funeral and I expected to confront him again when I walked through the door. He would be there in the faint but clinging smell of blood, the sinister shape of knives.

But there was nothing to suggest that I had returned to the killer's nest. The rooms were neat and warm and silent. The Sandman had left the Mackerel. When I bought the newspapers I found that even they had discovered new heroes and villains to thrill their readers. Some mad African dictator had crushed an insurgence by decapitating the rebel leader and eating him in public. The French had killed a thousand people with poisoned rice sent to Bangladesh as famine relief. The Chinese had found a cure for cancer that was so potent it killed those it cured. The murder hunt had been almost forgotten.

It would have been easy to kill again. It was the perfect moment. But I was lethargic. I was not anxious to shake the Sandman from his slumber. The knowledge that I alone possessed the power to wake this strange figure and set him loose in the London streets gave me a particular pleasure. And while this pleasure lasted, it was not necessary to kill again.

I spent my time in the Charing Cross Road, searching for conjuring books. In the evenings I brought out my scrapbook and studied my collection of Polaroids.

I wrote to Dorothy and thanked her for all the help she had

given me but I did not receive a reply. It surprised me. She had been unusually silent during my visit and, although it might have been the funeral that had upset and depressed her, I wondered if I might have offended her without knowing it. I cannot pretend to understand women. The oddest things upset them.

I should have understood the warning. I should have done something. But, at the time, I dismissed it. I could not guess, I could not know, that I would never see her again.

I had not woken up long enough to make myself coffee when there was a knocking on the door. When I opened it I found Johnson Johnson standing there in a scarlet quilted dressing-gown and black leather slippers. He looked terrible. His face was scrubbed raw and his wet hair pasted thinly across his scalp. His eyes were still yellow with sleep.

"Good morning, Mr Burton," he said with a smile.

"What's the problem, Johnson – is your mother complaining again?" I asked impatiently.

Johnson Johnson looked hurt. "My mother is fine, thank you," he said and flared his nostrils at me.

"Oh."

"Her liver is bad, but she's not in pain," he corrected quickly, anxious not to give me the impression that she had made any miraculous recovery.

"Good," I said, nodding my head and frowning in a concerned manner.

Johnson Johnson was encouraged by my interest. "She's not a strong woman," he confided, "I dread to think what would happen if I wasn't here to look after her. . .if I broke a leg or caught something infectious. . ."

"There are some very good nursing homes," I ventured.

"Good God, it would be criminal to send her away. It would be murder. She wouldn't survive a week in one of those places," he gasped.

"Yes, I expect you're right," I mumbled in apology.

There was an uncomfortable silence until Johnson Johnson held out his hand,

"It's a letter for you," he explained, "It came through our door by mistake. . .the address is very badly written."

"Thank you," I said in surprise. I took the envelope and turned it over in my fingers. It was small, square and very crumpled.

"It's nothing," said Johnson Johnson with another smile, "We've always thought of you as more of a friend than a neighbour." It was plainly nonsense and yet, glancing at him, I could see he was sincere. I felt slightly ashamed of myself.

"I hope it's not bad news," he said.

"No, I don't think it's anything important," I said, pinching the envelope in an effort to feel the contents. I could not recognise the handwriting or the postmark. It was a mystery.

"Ah, good," said Johnson Johnson without moving, "Good." He was waiting for me to open it and read it aloud.

"Well, thanks again," I said and gently closed the door on him.

"It was no trouble," he called as he loitered outside on the stairs.

I carried the envelope into the kitchen and laid it on the table where I could watch it while I made the coffee. When I finally tore it open I was shocked to discover it was a letter from Wendy Figg. A single pink page of thin handwriting. I don't know how she managed to find my address and I couldn't decide if my shock was pleasure or fright. As soon as I glanced at the spidery signature at the foot of the page my first thought, even after so many years, was that she had decided to try and prosecute me for assault.

The last time I had seen Figg she had been sprawled on the bed with her nightdress thrown over her head, more dead than alive, waiting for me to plunder her fat and secret places. But she made no mention of it in her letter. Her memories were carefully chosen and mostly concerned with my mother. She had heard of the old lady's death through the local newspaper and was anxious to send me her sympathies.

There was a paragraph or two about her own life and times. It didn't amount to very much – but she had never expected to become the Queen of Persia. She had married a television repair man and settled down to live in the house next to her mother. She was raising a family. The boy was called Burma and the girl, Bermuda. Fancy names for dull children. She said she was happy and there was no reason to doubt it.

As I sat and drank the coffee I tried to conjure her up in my head. She had always been the size of a sofa but she would be even bigger now, of course, than when I had last tried to peep between the buttons of her nylon coat. She would be swollen fit to burst her seams. The yellow bunches of hair would be cut and curled into some more sensible fashion for the kitchen. Ah, but she could never lose that brittle, porcelain face, the puckered mouth and surprised stare. Sweet Figg.

I was so excited by her letter that I wanted to drive down to the coast without delay and visit her at home. I wanted to hide in the bushes of her little garden and peer through her windows as she sliced bread and wiped noses, boiled cabbage and scrubbed floors. More. I would creep into her bed under cover of darkness and fire again my childhood passion. No, that was an idle fantasy. The bed would be crowded with husband and children. I would drive down and kidnap my Figg, bind her by the hands and feet and carry her back to the safety of the apartment. A blindfold for the eyes and something to stifle her mouth. Figg wrapped into a living parcel and my address stamped on it. She would live in handcuffs at the end of my bed and I would feed her dainty morsels with a silver fork. No, it was too complicated. Swifter and neater to visit her at home, allow the knives to whisper sweet nothings into her ears and let the Polaroid kidnap her for me.

Yes, the camera could capture the living body of Figg where I would certainly fail. A hundred perfect photographs mounted in a leather album. The book of Figg. A magic picture book where she might dwell forever ripe and naked, beyond the withering touch of disease and old age. Figg had been the true inspiration for my first murder and she should be the inspiration for the last murder. There was poetry in it, I could see that quite clearly.

Well, all these thoughts amused me for a time but my elation gradually turned sour. Despite all her erotic magnetism, Figg reminded me of the hotel and the innocence of those early days. I thought again of my mother and found myself weeping. But not for several days did I learn how much more had been stolen from me.

The days before the storm were tranquil days, the mornings made mysterious by river mists and the afternoons warmed by the sanguine autumn light that fired the spires and rooftops of the city, burnt the tops of the trees in Hyde Park and washed down the broad, empty streets. For a brief season the city seemed to recapture something of its old imperial beauty. Victoria Station became a palace fit for a brace of princes and even Woolworth had a handsome glow, an oddly royal emporium.

I remember every movement I made in those last few days. Wednesday I went down to Oxford Street for a new pair of shoes. I had lunch in a little Indian restaurant behind Selfridges. In the afternoon I strolled along the Charing Cross Road and poked about in the bookshops but I did not buy anything. In the evening I watched television.

Thursday I walked along Vauxhall Bridge Road and stopped at Tachbrook's Tropical Fish Shop. I have often spent whole mornings just staring at their aquariums, it's one of my favourite haunts. You wouldn't believe the extraordinary kinds of life that can be found in a block of warm and bubbling water. There are fish like brilliant blue needles that move mysteriously in shoals, jerking back and forth as if they are stitching some invisible embroidery. There are invisible fish, delicate glass balloons so transparent you can see the twitching of their hearts and count their bones. Anyway, I stayed in Tachbrook's until the man behind the counter began to give me suspicious looks and then I walked as far as the Embankment and went into the Tate Gallery for coffee.

Friday I went to the market for vegetables and bought my groceries in Safeway. There was a clinging, grey mist creeping across from the Thames and I didn't stray far from home.

Saturday afternoon I went to the cinema to idle away a couple of hours. I watched a film about an orgy in a medieval nunnery. It began in an enormous wooden bathtub full of naked nuns and spilled over into the convent garden where a gardener was cutting cucumbers. The film was scratched to ribbons and the cinema, which was almost deserted, smelt of disinfectant and balding carpets. I was getting ready to leave, but while the leading lady was engaged in her unspeakable pursuit I realised that I recognised her face. There was no mistake. I had seen her somewhere in the past. That strange, bloated expression, the sly button eyes and the great dimpled buttocks: it was Nectarine Summers. They looked identical. I hadn't thought about my doll for years. It was an omen and I felt uneasy with the memory. I left before the film was finished and went back to the television.

Sunday I woke early and slipped out for newspapers. It had been raining and the streets were wet. I hurried back to the apartment, made some coffee and took the newspapers to bed. And it was there, sprawled in a warm bed with my head propped by pillows, that I learned the terrible news that Dorothy had been killed.

Archie had butchered her in a fit of jealousy. He had woken from a thick sleep and found her in the arms of another man. I don't remember his name. He was a stranger. Archie killed them both and then staggered, smothered in blood, from the house and disappeared. I read about it in the *News of the World*. The police found Dorothy in the kitchen freezer.

I felt numb. My fingers and toes went cold. I knew the newspaper report must be true but I refused to believe it. I crawled from the sheets and tried to telephone the house but when I dialled the number I heard nothing but a peculiar whistle in my ear. The telephone had been disconnected.

Dorothy's death infected my body like a disease. I was numb at first but it quickly thawed into terror. I forced my face into the pillows, hoping to die, choking on the feathers and dust. I ate aspirins in an effort to sleep but poisoned myself and threw up. I tried to recall our last moments together, the words we had spoken and all the secret glances, but I could remember nothing and cursed myself for it.

I thought of Archie running through the woods behind the house, screaming, eyes wild, his butcher's apron red with blood. Meat is life. Life is meat. Some men are born to be butchers. I was afraid he would try to reach me, knock on the door at midnight and beg me to shelter him. Two mad butchers hiding together in the wardrobe.

I wanted to weep. But the terror had started to make me shake and as I shook I began to laugh. It was a terrible, ghoulish laugh that seemed to bubble up from somewhere deep inside of me and I had no control over it. I laughed until the tears sprang from my eyes and stung my face. I laughed until my lungs were raw and my teeth hurt. I laughed. I laughed. I thought of Archie with his big, sad face and I laughed. I thought of Dorothy standing on tiptoe, lean and naked, and I laughed. I thought of the three of us standing together at my mother's graveside and I laughed again. All this time I thought I had been cheating Death of his pleasure and he had been flying in my shadow, cutting down the lives around me, snipping away at the threads of my world with his scissors. He had left me no one but Frank.

Finally, in the early hours of Monday morning, I hammered on Frank's door and fell, sobbing, into his arms. He was wearing green pyjamas. His face was soft and crinkled as a chestnut and his hair was damp from sleep.

"What's wrong?" he kept shouting at me in alarm, "What's wrong?" He was trying to push me away, hold me at arm's length to look at my face, but I clung to him grimly. I could not answer his question.

"Are you hurt?" he asked.

No. I managed to shake my head and reluctantly released my hold on him.

He took me into his apartment and guided me gently into an armchair. Then he gave me a glass of brandy and sat with me until I was calm enough to speak. While I gulped at the brandy a woman walked into the room. She was wearing a pillow. She had it pressed against her body like a small child and was trying to shelter behind it. Her face was swollen from sleep and bruised with smudges of lipstick and mascara. Her hair was a bright orange colour and stood on spikes on her head. I remember staring at her hair and thinking she must belong to some secret aboriginal tribe and my sobbing turned to giggling which must have frightened her because she ran away and stared at me from the safety of the bedroom.

"What's happening?" she called out in an angry voice.

"It's nothing to worry about," answered Frank softly, "It's a friend."

The woman seemed quite satisfied with his explanation and she returned a moment later wearing a sheet.

"Is he in trouble?" she asked as she knelt down beside the chair and stared at me with her mouth open.

"Yes," said Frank calmly.

"You want me to leave?" she asked him. She twisted her arm around his leg and began scratching at his pyjamas with her fingernails.

Frank glanced down at her and smiled apologetically.

"I'll get dressed," the woman muttered and returned to the bedroom. When she came out again she was wearing a long rabbit coat and a pair of silver shoes. Frank drew her into a corner and began to count out some money from his wallet. Then he kissed her lightly on the cheek and she left the premises without another word.

"I'm sorry," I said when she had gone, "I've driven your friend away."

"Don't be stupid," said Frank, "You can find friends like that on any street corner. Finish your brandy and then tell me your troubles." He pulled a pack of Camel from his pyjamas, poked two of them in his mouth and lit them together.

"I don't smoke, Frank."

"Give it a good suck," he smiled, "I'm trying to help."

So I sucked and coughed and tried to tell him about my mother's death and as much as I dared of my love for Dorothy. In a few short weeks I had lost everyone who cared for me. I cannot remember how much I told him. I wanted to tell him everything – although I could never have told him of Jane. He listened and nodded his head in sympathy, as I always knew he would when I needed him. He helped me back to my rooms and put me to bed.

"It hurts, Frank," I said.

"I know," he said. "I know. But the pain will burn itself out. Believe me." He threw the pack of Camel down on the table beside the bed.

"And I feel angry," I blurted out.

"It's natural to feel like that," said Frank, "Don't choke it back."

I stayed drunk for two days, burning my stomach with brandy and trying to cauterize the deeper wounds in my head. The butcher had swung his axe at little Dorothy but it was my blood that had rushed from her body and filled the carpet with its hot, thick perfume. As I lay in bed, stinking and starved, I was visited by terrible dreams. I dreamt I poisoned a reservoir and watched a whole city drink itself to death. I dreamt I set fire to hospitals and watched women suffocate in the ash and the smoke. Whatever I touched shrank and died beneath my hands. Wherever I dared to tread the land seemed to crumble beneath my heel.

I cannot find the words to describe the agony of those days and even if I could I would not share them with you. But gradually I recovered my senses and it was Johnson Johnson who finally brought me back from the land of the dead. I was sprawled in a drunken sleep in front of the television late one night when he started banging on my door with his fists. When I flung the door open he was standing there smiling with his arms folded over his chest.

"What's happening?" I mumbled.

"Mr Burton, my mother is trying to sleep. She has a very bad headache. Will you please turn down the noise of your television?"

"No. Go away," I demanded. I was confused with sleep and not prepared to recite the usual apologies and good wishes he had come to expect from me.

"I beg your pardon?" he said as he exchanged the smile for a sneer.

"Why don't you grow up and leave home? You're horrible. You give me the shivers," I explained.

He was shocked. He looked as if he'd just found a turd in his pocket.

"Now listen, you can't talk to me like that," he snapped.

"Sod off," I roared cheerfully.

"I'm warning you," he shouted, "I'm warning you." His face began to quiver and his nose began to swell. It was an extraordinary sight. I thought his nose might explode. It was nearly black with blood.

"Shut up, Johnson and go home. I'm tired of your stupid complaints. I can't even fart without waking up your mother."

He tried to find a suitable retort but words failed him. He took a step forward and prodded me in the ribs with his thumb. He was standing so close I could hear him grinding his teeth.

"You're a nasty specimen. I'm surprised they didn't drown you when you were born," I whispered.

He made a grab at my collar but I was too fast for him. I stepped on his foot and caught his nose in my fingers, twisting it hard against his face.

He screeched. His nose burst and a necklace of small red beads spilled across his shirt. He covered his nose in his hand and stared at me in horror. The beads fell through the cracks in his hand and bounced softly onto his shoes.

"I shall fetch the police," he shouted. "I shall have you investigated. You haven't heard the last of me. You'll live to regret it."

"If I find you outside my door again, I'll kill you," I shouted at him.

"I shall tell the police," he howled as he smeared at the blood on his shirt.

I shrugged off his threats and slammed the door in his face. I believe he took my grief with him when he ran down the stairs for there were no bad dreams for me that night. I enjoyed a sweet and silent sleep.

The next day I woke up determined to return to work and not sit at home wringing my hands and thinking of the past. If Death wanted to play games with me I was ready to meet the challenge. I would turn London into a knacker's yard, gutters would run scarlet, sewers would be choked with bones.

For a few days the weather was against me but as soon as the storms cleared I prepared my equipment and threw it into the Volkswagen. I was going to explore the territory south of the Thames and late one evening I set off, driving like a madman, in the direction of Battersea. A few minutes later I was lost among long terraces of dirty Victorian houses and I parked the car and began to walk. The streets were busy. I didn't care. I slipped through a garden gate and walked to the back of one of the houses. There was a single light burning in one of the attic windows but the lower rooms were in darkness, so I pulled on my gloves and tried the lock on the door. To my surprise the door swung open. It was careless to leave the door unlocked – an invitation to all manner of thief. I walked into the kitchen and waited for my eyes to adjust to the gloom.

It was a large modern kitchen that smelt of nothing but machines and cats. A freezer rumbled in the darkness. A clock on the wall muttered to itself as I passed beneath. I tiptoed across the room and made my way down a short corridor to the staircase. The stairs creaked. Beneath my tread each board gave a little groan of complaint. I drew a knife from my bag, afraid that I might be discovered before I had finished the climb. But I reached the attic in safety. Nonetheless my heart was pounding and I was surprised by a trickle of sweat down my neck. I was frightened. I had been careless in selecting the scene of my crime and too hasty in my approach.

It was dark at the top of the stairs but a thin slice of yellow light marked the door of the room I had glimpsed from the garden. I reached out towards the door but I could not push my hand against it. My mouth had turned dry. Who hid in that room? Who stood so silently on the other side of the door? Every time I stole into a house I was gambling that I could overcome the residents by force. But what would happen if I opened the door to be confronted by a madman with a knife? I had been lucky, yes, in the past. But my luck could turn and I wouldn't know until it was too late to make my escape.

I stood there in the dark, knife in glove, and scared myself with thoughts of murder. I had not yet made a bad mistake but that was no comfort. The success I had enjoyed in the past would only serve to make me careless in the future. Who was hiding behind that damned door? I should have taken the trouble to watch and wait before I went creeping up unknown flights of stairs.

I kicked out with my foot and burst through the door with a horrible shout. There was a woman sitting in a bath. As I slithered across the bathroom on soapy tiles the woman began to shout and plunge about in the water. She stood up to confront me and then jackknifed, trying to hide her body in her hands. I hit the wall with my shoulder and tried to compose myself. The woman returned to the water to hide. She sank beneath the surface leaving nothing exposed but her head and a pair of fat and steaming knees. The water was apple-green and full of bubbles.

"Good evening," I said as soon as I had recovered my breath.

"Don't be frightened," she replied in a terrified whisper, "I'm a social worker." She had small pointed ears and her hair was tied in a knot on the top of her head.

"What?"

"I'm a social worker," she whispered, "I can help. Don't move. Put your knife on the shelf and pass me that towel. We'll talk about it."

"You must think I'm crazy."

"No. . .I don't think *anyone* is crazy."

I slithered dangerously across the floor and squatted down beside the bath while she watched me with a critical eye. She thought I was a customer. A casualty of circumstance, the family or the street. She thought I was a victim but I proved her wrong. The knife sprang into her ear and the water changed colour. She stared at the crimson bubbles with an amazed expression on her face. She stopped talking. She tried to scoop up the bubbles in her hands. Her head was sinking very slowly beneath the surface.

I went outside to recover my camera. But when I returned there was nothing left of her head but the thick knot of hair standing up through the bubbles like a tropical plant. I pulled the plug to drain the bath and then took my pictures. She was a large social worker. There was a tiny pool of pink water caught in the centre of her belly. I gripped the edge of the bath with my hands, leaned forward and prodded the puddle with my tongue. It tasted of soap and perfume and blood. The Sandman drank and drew strength.

The following evening I took a bus as far as Oxford Circus and then walked down Poland Street, across Broadwick Street and into Berwick Street. It was a cold night but the place was bustling with tarts and tourists, drunks and deviants. I enjoyed the noise and movement of the streets. In Soho everyone is a stranger and the crowds sheltered me.

I walked towards Old Compton Street. Here, between the peepshows and the massage parlours, in draughty arcades lit by the glare of neon tubes, sheltered from the street by battered screens, young men with baleful expressions studied spanking magazines or browsed uneasily among books on boys, bondage and bestiality. Old men in crumpled coats peered at handcuffs and rubber masks and dreamed of tormenting their neighbours' daughters. Tourists smirked and shuffled their feet.

A team of Chinese waiters trotted past, dreaming of the mahjong tables waiting for them in the mysterious back rooms of Gerrard Street. An old Greek grocer watched them pass, pulled a damp cigar from his mouth and spat thickly against the wall. A cat, nesting in a pile of rubbish, stood up, shivered, and crossed the street in disgust.

A drunk came towards me. He was wrapped in a kind of shawl made from a sheet of black polythene and fastened at the neck with string. Beneath the shawl he was wearing a suit of shapeless rags that stank of sherry and urine. He tried to say something to me, jerking his head back and forth like a chicken, but the words were hopelessly slurred. I slipped my hand into my bag and showed him a knife. He turned and stumbled away. Drunks are sometimes killed for sport but I've never considered them worth my time. Drunks and drug fiends are the walking dead of the city. When he was safely out of sight I stepped into a tobacconist's doorway and studied the postcards in the window. 'Young model seeks driving post', 'Dainty butterfly needs mounting'. The invitations boldly scrawled in coloured crayons, each bearing its own telephone number. I pulled out a little notebook and discreetly copied down some of the numbers for future reference. A list of the living for the book of the dead.

I was walking along Shaftesbury Avenue towards Piccadilly Circus when, quite suddenly, I felt as if someone was following me. It was such a distinct feeling that I paused to glance over my shoulder. The street was almost deserted. A couple ran, hand in hand, towards the Apollo Theatre, late for the final performance. The man was singing. The woman was laughing. Their breath trailing like smoke in the frosty air. A drunk staggered from a doorway and stood in the gutter where he stared at his feet. Beyond the drunk, at the corner of Wardour Street, a group of young men stood watching the traffic lights change colour. No one was watching me. No one moved in my direction. I shivered and hurried away.

When I reached Piccadilly Circus I clattered into the Underground and rode as far as Hyde Park Corner, then I walked quickly home through Grosvenor Place. It was not until I had almost reached my door that I sensed again that I had been watched or followed. But this time I did not stop to look around. I ran into the apartment and locked the door. I ran across the room and almost fell against the window, peering down at the street, hoping to catch some glimpse of a retreating phantom. But there was nothing.

I made myself some hot milk and sat nursing it while I chuckled at my fear of the dark. I was feeling nervous, I had lost control of my imagination. The hunter felt hunted. It was natural. It was nothing to worry about. But even then, on that first evening, I knew the Sandman was no longer safe on the streets.

The next day I took a trip to Church Street market, wandered up and down the street, picking through the most dreadful corners of the poorest stalls where trays of bent spoons, cracked mirrors, dentures, spectacles, rusty scissors, torn books and chewed pencils were mixed together in piles of filthy rubbish. I spent a long time selecting the items that I thought might prove valuable: three pairs of greasy spectacles and a tiny cardboard drum of French rouge that was old and crusty. I earned some strange glances as I browsed so carefully through the rubbish but I didn't give a damn, because the next time I walked out in the street no one would recognise me. Death might stare me in the face but I would learn to disappear.

I drove back to Victoria and went into Woolworth where I bought a can of Funcolor hair spray – the stuff that sprays in and washes out. I couldn't decide between the red and the black so I bought the silver. Then I hurried home to construct my disguise.

I experimented with the rouge, working it into my cheeks, and across my nose, but the effect was luminous and alarming. I washed it off and abandoned the idea. The lenses were very thick in two pairs of the spectacles and, wearing them, I couldn't see my hand in front of my face. But the third pair was perfect. Behind the heavy frames my face felt diminished and protected. The Sandman was beginning to disappear.

The following day I turned to my notebook and rang one of the numbers. A woman answered and told me her name was Tulip. I made inquiries and, after a little hesitation, she gave me a list of her prices. I thought it was very expensive but then, as I had no intention of paying them, I agreed to her terms. I made an appointment to visit and she gave me her address. It was not, as I had supposed, a street in Soho, but a room in Wilton Road. She conducted her business just a few yards from Victoria Station.

I spent some time selecting my knives and dusting my old rubber gloves. I loaded the Polaroid with a fresh pack of film. I felt happy and excited again. My hands trembled as I packed my bag. It was marvellous. At dusk I took a warm bath, dressed carefully and prepared myself for the pleasures of the night. I combed my hair in the wrong direction and sprayed it with Funcolor silver. The spray filled my scalp with something that looked like aluminium talcum powder, a dull metal colour that flashed like silver whenever I moved my head to the light.

When I fitted the spectacles onto my nose even I had difficulty recognising myself in the mirror.

At ten-thirty precisely I locked my apartment, tiptoed down the stairs and strolled with a smile into Wilton Road. I turned into a doorway beside a Turkish restaurant, walked up a narrow, unlit flight of stairs and knocked on a heavy door. There was music coming faintly from the Turkish restaurant and a faraway smell of hot, spicy food.

A woman answered the door. She looked plump, pampered and gave off a heavy scent of flowers. She was wearing a black satin dress, high-heeled mules and an absurd wig of thick treacle curls that fell, in glittering cascades, to her elbows. Beneath the wig her face seemed very small and flat. She had the eyes of a goldfish and a slightly crooked mouth. Her eyebrows were no more than tiny black brushstrokes and her lips a mere splash from a scarlet pen.

She beckoned me silently into the room and carefully closed the door.

"What shall I call you?" she asked as she turned to inspect me.

"My name is William," I said.

"That's nice. I'll call you Billy."

I felt awkward standing there in the middle of the room clutching my leather bag in my hands. She seemed to sense my embarrassment and smiled.

"Don't look so scared, Billy. I'm not going to eat you," she chirruped. She seemed to think this was a huge joke and began to laugh. I couldn't understand it. She just stood there and laughed. When she saw that I was not amused she tried to compose herself. She lit a cigarette, gave it several brief tugs and snorted smoke through her nose. Her hands were fat, the fingernails square and painted red.

"Why don't you sit down, Billy, and take off your coat?"

"Thank you," I said. I took off my coat and folded it over the bed. I sat down and glanced at a door behind me. I couldn't work out where the door might lead, other rooms perhaps, a fire escape or the restaurant kitchens. I bobbed my head, hoping to squint through the keyhole but the spectacles distorted my view.

"That's my own private room, Billy," she said, "Would you like a drink?"

"Is it empty?" I asked.

"Yes, of course it's empty. *This* is the room where I entertain. Don't worry, Billy, we're quite alone. Be brave and have a drink."

"Yes," I said, "Thank you."

"Scotch?"

"Fine," I said.

She turned to pour me a drink from a cabinet beside the bed.

"I haven't seen you before," she said.

"No," I said.

"Is this your first time?"

I nodded my head.

"That's nice," she said. "Well, don't look so unhappy. You'll be fine. I've got clients who've been coming here for years and years. You'd be surprised. They're just like old friends. They look after me and I take care of them. You understand?"

I nodded and sipped at the Scotch. She sat down on the edge of the bed and crossed her legs. A bracelet of silver beads flashed on her ankle. She smiled and tugged at her cigarette. Through the shroud of smoke her eyes flickered across my face, my hands, my clothes, my shoes.

"Some girls don't care. They work the streets, steal your money while you're pressed against a wall with your pants around your knees. They give the business a bad name. I like to make my clients feel special. That's why I've gone to so much trouble here. It always pays to take a little extra trouble." She gestured around the room with a fat, white hand.

The room was small and very hot. An aluminium blind with candy-coloured slats had been lowered against the window. On a shelf above the basin a bowl crammed with tablets of scented soap. A cheap glass vase of wilting roses on a low metal table. A wardrobe. Rugs on the floor. A telephone beside the bed. Several dolls on a narrow bookshelf.

"I used to be a dancer," she explained, "I've had classical training. But I have very weak ankles. . ."

Without warning she opened her dress at her throat and

peeled it away from her shoulders and breasts. There was a pause in the undressing while she searched for an ashtray, picked it up, dropped it, picked it up and stabbed it several times with her cigarette. Then she prised her fingers into the wrinkled satin that had bunched around her belly and pushed the dress to her knees. It fell whispering to her feet and she stepped out of it with a little wave of her hand and a smile. She was wearing nothing but a pair of fine black stockings that cut wickedly into the top of her thighs making the skin there seem excessively polished and fat. Her breasts were heavy and swung loosely when she moved. The nipples were small as buttons. She dipped her hand between her legs and tweaked at the hair between finger and thumb, twisting it into a long black curl. She did not seem disturbed by the stranger who sat and stared at her from the safety of the armchair. She lit another cigarette and then perched on the arm of my chair, swinging her leg, rubbing her breasts against my face.

"There, Billy, isn't that nice?" she inquired. She tugged at the cigarette, threw back her head and blew smoke towards the ceiling.

The heat of her body, the slack, voluptuous weight of her breasts against my face, aroused me to a fever of excitement. I trembled. Yes. I stiffened and burned. But I was not aroused in the manner of other men. I would not penetrate and possess her in the manner of all the other men who had sat in that chair and taken the nipple between their teeth.

As she fumbled with the buckle of my belt I reached up and whispered in her ear.

"I wonder if you would allow me to indulge in a little habit of mine. . .?"

Tulip stopped playing with my belt and stood away from the chair.

"What is it?" she asked suspiciously, "I don't want anything violent. And I don't do anything – you know – dirty. This is a nice place." She tugged in frustration at her cigarette.

"Oh, no, it's nothing unpleasant," I said soothingly, "But I'd feel much happier if I could wear my gloves."

She frowned and shrugged.

"They seem to lend me so much more confidence. I suppose it's the rubber. They have such a wonderful rubbery smell."

"Yeah, but what are you going to do with them?" she demanded darkly.

"Wear them," I smiled innocently, afraid that she might have some more extraordinary experience of rubber gloves.

As I reached into the leather bag for the gloves I slipped a knife up my sleeve with the sly movement of a conjurer's deceit. The blade was cold against my skin. It made me shiver with delight. I turned again to Tulip and offered my gloves for her approval. She wrinkled her nose but said nothing. I began to roll the gloves onto my hands, kneading and poking them between my fingers.

"What else have you got in that bag?" she asked, bending towards it.

"Books," I said absently.

"I read a book once," she said and crushed out her cigarette.

Then the Sandman held out his arms and bade the Tulip approach. She smiled and stepped forward, pressing herself against him. He shook his sleeve and the blade sprang like magic into his hand.

As she sank deeper into the embrace I dragged her forward and let her collapse softly into the chair. A chrysanthemum of blood had blossomed in her ear. I stepped back and stared. She was sprawled as if asleep, her arms hanging loose and her legs slightly parted. The stockings were wrinkled and torn loose from their moorings. Her head rested against one shoulder. She stared at me sweetly.

I knelt down and tried to smooth the stockings against her knees but the gloves made me clumsy and I dragged them down in exasperation and peeled them from her toes.

I stared up at the woman and smiled blissfully. I was very happy. She wore the handle of the knife against her hair in the manner of a Japanese comb. The chrysanthemum had thickened and its petals were spreading against her neck. I stretched out my hand and touched her face tenderly with my bright rubber fingertips. I closed her eyes and her mouth fell open. Her tongue was as red as a pomegranate. I brushed the hair away from her breasts and arranged her hands in her lap. She had lost her mules and I retrieved them, neatly slipping them onto her feet.

When I was satisfied with her appearance I took my leather bag from beneath the armchair and pulled out the Polaroid. I took three pictures of the woman and laid the prints along the edge of the bed. I peered at the pictures anxiously, impatient to examine their detail.

And then I heard it. A scuffle, a muffled cough, a groan or a sigh. I don't know – I cannot say exactly what I heard – but I felt someone was watching me! I turned in horror towards the window and stared at the cracks in the metal blind. I swung towards the chair and I snarled at the door. Oh God, I was frightened nearly to death. I began to wet my pants – I suppose it was the shock, the sudden alarm that made me lose control. But I managed to check myself, hold my breath and swallow the yawning fear in my throat. I could not see the face that concealed itself so cleverly but I could feel it watching me.

Nothing moved. If I had stumbled into a trap there would have been the clatter of boots and the shouts of surrender and arrest. But there was only the silence. Whoever was watching me had stumbled by accident upon my terrible secret. Whoever was hiding there in the room must have taken his own pleasures from the withered Tulip. I twisted on my heels and scooped the pictures from the bed. I threw the photographs, the camera and the empty tumbler into the open leather bag, bundled my coat beneath my arm and ran from the room.

As I scampered down the dark corridor of stairs into the glare of the busy street I struggled to pull off my gloves and pull on my coat. I turned blindly into Wilton Road and began to walk as fast as my legs would carry me towards the Thames. I was too frightened to return to the apartment. I remember reaching the Embankment and, saving nothing but the Polaroids, hurling my precious leather bag into the filthy water.

When I turned I saw a figure standing, watching me, from the far side of the street. He looked like Archie. His head was tilted on his shoulder and he stared without blinking, stared at me with tears in his eyes. I was confused. I thought he had come to take me to the slaughter house. I thought he had come to take me to Dorothy's grave. I wanted to open the freezer where Dorothy had been lain to rest and sleep beside her on her bed of ice. I shouted his name but he did not answer. He continued to stare. Then he pulled his hands from his pockets, big, butcher's hands with ugly raw knuckles and began to walk towards me.

I ran for my life, along the Embankment, across Vauxhall Bridge and into the unknown streets of Lambeth. At midnight or beyond, weeping with cold, I stumbled into a café to buy a few minutes' warmth. I was lost and too tired to walk any more. I ordered a coffee and sat with it at the steamy warmth of a window table where I could keep a stealthy watch on the street.

I reached for the coffee but as I raised the cup to my mouth I caught sight of blood on my sleeve. A purple gobbet of Tulip's blood. I dropped the cup in horror, fled the café and staggered home to hide.

Chapter Four

He stopped reading. The diary was finished. There were several blank pages which he thumbed idly before he snapped the book shut. How long had he been crouched at the table? He squinted at his wristwatch. It was a little after four in the morning. His fatigue had distilled into a small pain behind his eyes. His shoulders ached.

He ripped open the Camel pack and recovered the last cigarette which he gripped, rigid, between his teeth. He crept across the room and pressed his face against the door, his ear crushed cold against the wood, listening for the slightest sound. Through the whispering complaints of his own blood he fancied he could detect voices calling his name, distant laughter and footsteps on the stairs.

He rummaged through the litter on his desk and teased out a narrow strip of paper. Gently, holding the scrap between finger and thumb, he rubbed the paper smooth. There was a telephone number on the paper. If he dialled the number it would lead him to the murder enquiry desk. A direct line to his own police confessional, twenty-four hours a day. He had copied the number from a newspaper report and, although the number was already etched in his memory, he read it again and recited it aloud.

The sound of his own voice startled him. He knew, for the sake of sanity, he must telephone the police and surrender. He must not hesitate. He picked up the phone and dialled the number. His palms were cold and slippery with sweat. He pressed the receiver against the side of his skull as if it were a loaded pistol. He held his breath, listening to the number ring. And then a voice challenged him. He asked for the murder desk, there was a pause and a second voice demanded his name and address. He could not speak. He was weeping. When they asked his business he whispered the Sandman's name and address. Again they asked for identification and again he whispered the Sandman's name. Then he replaced the receiver and sat down to wait.

Chapter Five

This is the final entry I shall make in my little journal. The police came yesterday to question me about the killings.

I answered the door and found two of them standing outside in the shadows. One was fat as an owl with a short, hooked nose the colour of garlic sausage. His hair was cropped too close against his skull and his ears, which were thick and very crumpled, seemed to sprout from his face like a pair of rudimentary wings. He was wearing a stainless steel wristwatch and a diamond ring. The other was a slightly younger man with a lumpy yellow face. His eyes were an extraordinary shade of blue and so pale that, when he entered the light, he looked quite blind. There were traces of a purple rash around his chin. The work of a blunt razor.

"Is your name William Burton?" asked the fat one in a flat voice.

"Yes."

"I wonder if we might ask you a few questions, sir?" asked the younger one.

"Yes, of course," I said and ushered them into my room. They stood in the middle of the carpet and stared in different directions. When I invited them to sit down and make themselves comfortable they perched together on the edge of the sofa.

"We've received a particular telephone call containing a very serious allegation. . ." the fat one said slowly.

"How can I help you?" I enquired, sitting down in my armchair, folding my hands in my lap.

"During this particular telephone call your name was given as that of a particular man we are seeking to help us with our enquiries concerning a particular number of serious crimes. . ." The fat police officer pronounced each word very carefully, as if he were speaking a foreign language.

"But that's terrible," I gasped.

"I'm sure it's nothing to worry about but, as I'm sure you understand, we have to investigate every incident, no matter how trivial," said the young officer with the lumpy yellow face. He smiled and exposed a set of very large teeth.

"Do you live here alone, sir?" asked the fat one.

"Yes."

"Very nice. Very comfortable. Very clean and tidy," he said, as if reading from a phrase book.

"Thank you," I said.

"May I ask what you do for a living, sir?" asked the young one.

"I'm a kind of historian – I'm writing a book about conjuring."

"Cutting women in half."

"Yes." I smiled a broad and innocent smile.

"It must be very difficult to make money from writing."

"Yes." I frowned slightly.

"Have you had anything published?"

"No. I have a small private income – enough to buy the groceries."

"Very useful. Very nice."

"I wonder if you could tell us where you were on the night of the 15th, sir?"

I frowned and nodded and thought back to the night of Tulip's death.

"It was last Sunday night," said the one with the lumpy yellow face helpfully.

"I don't know if I was doing anything special – I usually spend my evenings at work." I gestured around the room at my books.

"It would help if you could try and remember if there was anything unusual. . ."

I shrugged. "Wasn't that the night the Butcher killed that poor woman in. . ."

"Yes, sir."

"But. . .you're not here in search of *him*? Are you?"

There was a moment's silence. The two policemen stared at me without expression.

"That's terrible," I exploded with a nervous laugh.

The fat one began rubbing his nose, bending the sausage back and forth against his face.

"Oh, don't worry – it's just part of the routine," he said, "If it's any comfort. . ." He stopped talking and teased a grey handkerchief from his trouser pocket, shook it a few times, wrapped it around the sausage and gave a long, wet snort. "You don't even fit the description," he concluded with a gasp.

I was fascinated. "So you know who you're looking for at last?" I gently prompted. "You have a description?"

He's a big black man. Twenty-five, thirty years old. Probably married with a couple of kids."

"But he's a monster," I protested.

"Oh, yes. He's certainly a monster. But monsters are strange animals, sir. When he's not roaming the streets poking knives into women's ears he's probably as normal as the next man. We think he works in a factory or something similar."

"But his wife must know. . ." I said.

"You'll be surprised," said the fat one.

"I expect he'll kill himself before we manage to get our hands on him. They often do that," added his companion sadly.

"You mean he'll commit suicide?" I asked.

"Yes. The crazy ones usually end up destroying themselves."

"But how will you know if he's dead?"

"Simple. We'll know he's dead when the killings stop."

"Would you like a cup of coffee?" I said.

"Thank you," they said.

I strolled into the kitchen and switched on the kettle. It was impossible to imagine how they had reached the conclusion that the killer was a black man with a wife and family to support and I was hardly in a position to argue with them. But I was quite shaken by the news. I made the coffee, fresh, in a stone jug, and arranged a few biscuits on a plate. My favourite biscuits – Godfrey's Fingers. I arranged everything on a tray and, when I felt strong enough to face them again, carried the tray to my guests.

We sat and sipped the coffee and discussed the alarming increase in violent crimes.

"It's frightening," I said, "We could all be murdered in our beds."

The fat one sympathised with me, "We're too soft on villains," he said, "I'm old fashioned. I believe in giving them a good thrashing."

The one with the lumpy yellow face picked up one of Godfrey's Fingers and sniffed it suspiciously. Tiny flakes of sugar clung to the tip of his nose. He dipped the biscuit into his coffee and sucked it smoothly into his mouth.

"A proper flogging under medical supervision," dreamed the fat one.

"It wouldn't stop these killings," argued his companion, "It wouldn't stop the loonies."

"That's true," said the owl mournfully.

"But who could have made such a terrible phone call?" I said, anxious to remain the centre of conversation. "Who could hate me enough to accuse me of those horrible murders."

"I wouldn't lose any sleep over it. We get dozens of hoax phone calls. Whoever it was probably picked your name from the telephone directory. It happens."

"We get crazy kids wandering into the station actually claiming to *be* the killer."

"That's horrible," I murmured, shaking my head.

The fat one looked pleased. He poked a Godfrey's Finger into his mouth and snapped it between his teeth. "There's a killer in everyone," he declared philosophically.

"And a victim," added the one with the lumpy yellow face, gently wiping his fingers around his chin, "But I'll never understand them."

At last they stood up and moved towards the door. Then they turned, apologised for disturbing me, and said goodbye.

It was an exorcism. In the past few weeks I had begun to haunt myself and now the ghost had been driven out. I had sweated in my bed at night, startled awake by dreams of surrender, delivering myself into the hands of the executioner, only to discover my own face staring back at me. I had walked to the very heart of that dark forest where the hunters are taken to stalk themselves. And now I had been returned to the daylight. I had given the police my name and address, invited them to arrest me for my crimes. And they had come tiptapping at my door, cap in hand, and declared me to be an innocent man.

I mixed myself a stiff drink and went and sprawled on the sofa. It was an exorcism. I had sneezed the Sandman from my body. He had exploded into a million particles and was free to settle wherever he desired. He was an unknown black man working at a factory bench. He was a crazy man with a head full of whisky who pleads with the police to bully and beat him. He was the secret fantasy of a thousand young men who dream of power over women. It was an exorcism and a ritual cleansing. I was free of my sorrow. I was free to be another man and conduct some other kind of life.

Before I went to bed I brought out my scrapbook and reviewed my work. I curled up in a nest of cushions, sipped a scalding mug of milk and studied each precious Polaroid. Here was Patsy, grinning from ear to ear, sitting on Jumbo's hairy knees and Jumbo himself, grinding his teeth and rolling his eyes like a demented Buddha. They might have been father and daughter or an old ventriloquist and his overgrown doll. It was only the peculiar sight of the Buddha's knees wrapped together in a towel that suggested he was staring death between the eyes.

Here were Hammersmith housewives still in their kitchens with their mouths open and their eyes closed. And Marlene from New South Wales sitting on the floor in her party frock, her blood spread across the frock like a shadow, her breast hanging from the shadow like a paper lantern.

I peered again at the Hornet Sisters as they made their farewell public appearance. They looked a lot less like corpses in death than they had in life. The frail and wrinkled faces had begun to unravel and relax. They looked quite happy to be gone. In the darkness beyond the old ladies a cat stared out at the camera with cadmium yellow eyes.

Here was the social worker blushing brightly pink from her recent blood bath. And finally Tulip, the magnificent Tulip, wilted but still beautiful as she sat in her chair and displayed her legs. I laid out the Polaroids on the table, kissed them each in their turn and went to bed.

It is finished. And yet, writing these words, I know that death is my life and death will be the end of me. I have, several times, thought of throwing this diary in the river. But I cannot bring myself to destroy it. I have followed death as he knocked on doors and introduced himself. I have helped him in his most difficult labours. We have become intimate friends. I cannot leave him now, after everything we've shared, shake his hand and walk away. Death follows me everywhere. Death tiptoes from my wardrobe in the darkest moments of the night, crawls on his belly through cracks in the woodwork, spirals down chimneys and wriggles through keyholes. Death places a knife in my hand while I dream and wakes me from sleep with the warm, elusive smell of blood.